CORMORANT
IN THE NET

Author of *Murder at Pelican Lake*

By Marjorie
Mathison Hance

North Lakes Press | Plymouth, MN 55442

ISBN: 9798541923728
Library of Congress Catalog Number: 2021915016
Printed in the United States of America
First Printing: 2021

Cover art by Pelican Rapids artist Marcella Rose
Illustration © Marcella Rose. All rights reserved.
www.marcellarose.com

Book design and typesetting by Dan Pitts.

North Lakes Press
10985 - 56th Avenue North
Plymouth, MN 55442
(952) 484-2824
northlakespress@gmail.com

To order: individual copies are available through Amazon.com, or contact North Lakes Press for bulk orders. Reseller discounts available.

Contact Marjorie Mathison Hance at mmhance4@gmail.com for speaking engagements, book club discussions, freelance writing projects, and interviews.

Cormorant in the Net is the second book in the North Lakes Mystery series. The third book, The Man Three Cottages Down is scheduled for release Spring, 2022. Book one, Murder at Pelican Lake, is available at amazon.com or by contacting North Lakes Press.

PROLOGUE

It was a beautiful Saturday morning. Blue sky. No wind. Still water. Temperature around 75 degrees. Perfect for an early September day. The smell of dead fish lingered in the air.

Fishing had been good. Adeptly steering his small trolling boat through an area where thick, vinelike weeds rose almost to the surface of the water, he was rewarded by another strike on his line. The islands submerged in the lake provided good structure for walleye to hide. Quickly netting a small, feisty northern, he added it to the stringer with the now-subdued 21-inch walleye and two largemouth bass he'd caught earlier. He would have a delicious fish dinner when he got back from Fargo tonight, succulent white fish meat, coated with the special seasoning he'd picked up in Lake Park. How he hated leaving the lake. Cormorant was so tranquil this time of the day. But he had no choice; he had to get back for the game late this afternoon. Revving the engine, he headed toward his dock, past the deserted YMCA camp. Maybe on his way back from Fargo he would stop at the local pub and get an order of their potato special to round out his meal. The thought of it made his mouth water.

As he drove into Fargo, forty minutes away, he was consumed by thoughts of the upcoming game. They were good enough to win against this team, but they had been playing terribly. What was with them? Hanna, the leader of his team, was probably the strongest. She was level-headed, calm under pressure, a real galvanizer. But the rest of them. What a discombobulated bunch. He'd have to recruit some new, hot freshmen for next year. This year was almost a lost cause, even this early in their season. Of course, he had Annie. Yes, she definitely had potential, he thought, a small smile creeping across his lips.

Entering the dark gym, he flipped the switch for the main bank of lights. The overhead scoreboard, now dim, cast a shadow across the floor. The smell of sweat wafted through the air, a scent that reminded him of hard work, competition, winning. He walked along the side of the volleyball court to the net.

Climbing onto the ref's stand gave him better access to the net. He had a lot of equipment to check and only an hour before the gym would begin to fill up. Because the stand felt a little wobbly, he leaned over to tighten the wingnuts on the bolts that secured the legs to the platform, fumbling with the protective foam that covered the structure. Suddenly a shadow catapulted toward him. He saw the massive scoreboard, dislodged from its mounting in the ceiling, careening straight toward him. When he tried to move quickly to avoid a blow, he found himself losing his balance. Just before the scoreboard hit him, he saw a human shape standing in the shadows, holding a rope, watching him silently. In a split second, he realized what was happening and knew this was not going to end well. The scoreboard struck him straight on, smashing his body into the side of the ref's stand, which gave way under his weight. He groaned as he slammed into the steel cable securing the net. His body flew into the net, coming abruptly to a halt. The world stopped instantly.

I

Monday afternoon

It was never a good sign when Mark Dolan dropped in on Carley unannounced. The last time he had was a month ago, when he had given her the difficult news that her father, who had died two years earlier, had actually been murdered. It had been a difficult time. Carley had come to Pelican Lake to regroup, not to get embroiled in even bigger drama. Life at the lake had now, seemingly, reverted to the idyllic calm she had always known there.

Well, almost reverted. She'd slept fitfully since the turmoil of the summer. She couldn't walk into the Bait Shop without shuddering. The abandoned storage units and semis in disrepair up the road were a constant reminder of the trial that was about to start up. And she made sure the door to her new garage was always locked. The way she'd started the summer—jobless, loveless, and homeless, except for her inherited cabin on Pelican Lake—hadn't changed. She still hadn't found her new life, a sense of direction, a path forward. The stirring sunsets, her welcoming neighbors on the beach, and the weekday solitude were helping her heal, but it hadn't been easy.

Carley took a deep breath and opened the door. "Good to see you…I hope?" she said, tentatively.

Mark stood smiling, dangling keys in front of her nose. Even though he was almost forty, six years older than she, an almost irrepressibly boyish grin flitted across his face, a contrast to his usually serious demeanor.

"What are those?" she pressed.

"The keys to my new lake home," he said, a gleam in his eyes. "I found a little place down the road from here. I just couldn't get Pelican Lake out of my blood."

If she were a squealer, Carley would have squealed. She was thrilled that Mark would be nearby, at least some of the time. They had become close during the events of the summer, and he had become like a brother to her. Instead, she gave him a big hug. "I didn't know you were looking for a place. What a great surprise! Well, can we go see it?" she asked.

"Of course," he said, chuckling.

Mark had used the Gallagher cottage a few doors down from hers as his stakeout base for the summer. She wasn't sure why, but she was relieved as they walked past that one. He was still on the same beach, just down the hill and around the bend. Close, but not too close. Maybe now she could sleep again. There was something reassuring about having him nearby.

His new cottage was a similar vintage to hers—small, rustic, wood fireplace, outdoor fire pit, knotty pine paneling. It needed some work—the paint around the trim was curling, the wood around a few windows was clearly deteriorating, and the walkway to the cabin had disintegrated. Carley chuckled to herself. She was probably handier at home repair than he was.

"Now I just have to find some time to come out here," he said, a little wistfully. She knew that would be a challenge. His FBI work made for long hours and a fair amount of travel, even if it was only in Minnesota and North Dakota. But she understood the magnetic pull of Pelican Lake. It was the place where she always felt most like herself. How ironic that she had run into a whole new set of challenges here.

Mark jiggled the key in the lock to open the door. "Not exactly the most modern place," he noted.

"Always the master of understatement," Carley commented drolly. "Actually, I love it. It's not very big, but you don't need a big place to manage. You need a place that lets you relax, be by the water, spend time outside. Plus, you have a great view. And look at that stone fireplace."

He nodded in agreement. From his cabin he could see the opening to Fish Lake, the eastern shore of Pelican, and the "castle" on the other side. Sunrise would be spectacular. The wooden bench on the inviting dock overlooked the bay. "I really fell in love with this area. I'll keep my condo in Fargo, but it isn't too far to commute to my office if I want."

Carley surveyed the dilapidated recliner, the card table that served as a temporary dining room table, and the worn rug by the fireplace. "So…it came fully furnished?" she laughed. "I could help with that."

"Really? That would be awesome. Decorating has never been my long suit. I don't have a lot to invest in furnishings, but I could come up with something."

"It's a deal. It's the least I could do since you very kindly saved my life."

He smiled. "That comes with the territory. You don't owe me a thing."

"I know that's what you think," she said. "But I would be thrilled to do something for you in return. I'm willing to give decorating a try, and I'm pretty frugal. After all, cabin chic is my specialty," she said, a little tongue-in-cheek, knowing she hadn't updated anything in her own, very rustic, log cabin.

Her phone buzzed in her pocket. As she pulled it out, she saw it was a number she didn't recognize. Probably a telemarketer, she thought. Glancing tentatively at Mark, who nodded, she answered it, heading for the doorway.

After a few minutes, she returned, looking rather surprised.

"Everything okay?" Mark asked.

"Yeah. That was the athletic director from my alma mater in Fargo. His volleyball coach died last night in a freak accident, and he asked if I'd come in and talk with him about helping out. It's midseason, so I'm sure it's hard to come by a coach."

"Aren't you lucky!" Mark said. "Looks like a job might have just fallen into your lap. I forgot you were a hotshot player in college. Weren't you captain of a national championship team?"

Carley laughed. "How did you know that? Yes, I was captain, but no, we took second place. We had a great team. The athletic director must be hoping that will translate into 'great coach.' I'm sure, at this point, he's just trying to save the season. It's hard to find an experienced coach in September. Everyone else is just getting underway. While it's not quite the career path I had in mind, I love volleyball and I could use a diversion about now. Come on. Let's go. I'll race you back to my place."

With that, she started off. Mark quickly joined in, and they fell into a comfortable run, around the corner, up the hill, and down the treelined road, until they reached her home, past the cottage three doors down of the man who, unbeknown to her, had watched Carley through his binoculars all summer.

2

Ten days before the Coach's death

Their first big tournament was about to get underway. They were play-ing their archrival, an outstate college with a solid record. Hanna studied the opposition carefully. At 5'8" she was a strong setter, the leader of her team, but the opponents were at least three—and some six—inches taller than she. As her team huddled, she said, "Don't be intimidated. They're big, but we're quick. We can do this."

The uneasy look in the players' eyes told her otherwise. But she had to try to rally the team. Isn't that the job of a team captain, after all? They'd been practicing for two months. She'd seen what they could do. As they huddled together, they wrapped their arms around each other's shoulders, shouting, "Team!" before they dispersed to their positions. Several held two fingers up behind their backs, a sign of their defensive strategy.

The opponent drilled a serve over the net. Juanita, who normally would be the one to get the ball into play, missed it. And the next serve. And the next serve.

Calling a timeout, the coach yanked Juanita over next to him. "What the hell is going on with you?" he hissed at her, leaning forward until he was almost nose to nose with her. "Can't you do anything right? You're out. Go over there." She backed away, grimacing, wiping his sprayed saliva off her face. He pointed to the bench with the others sit-ting on the sideline.

Stifling tears, Juanita took her place at the end of the bench. None of the others looked her in the eye, except Hanna, who left the huddle, came up, put her arm around her, and gave her a quick squeeze. "Don't lose the faith," she said calmly. "We'll get you back in. We need you." Of course, the coach had other ideas.

The play continued, with the women falling in each other's way. "The next time you don't call a ball, you're off the team," the coach sputtered.

Annie, a fairly green first year student, missed three hits in a row. Coach called a timeout. "You—I'll see you in my office when this is over," he said with venom in his tone, motioning the team back into play.

By the end of the first game, the entire starting team was benched, and the second string was in, trying to prove they could play at the level the coach expected, each of them desperately wanting a starting position. The misfortune of the six starters opened a door for them. Unfortunately, none of them walked through it. The pressure of performing and a coach agitatedly pacing were too much. With the score of 25-9 in the second game, the coach threw his hands up in desperation and walked off the court, leaving the players to fend for themselves in game three.

Later that evening, after they lost the final game 25 to 14, Annie made her way to the coach's office. "You wanted to see me?" she asked, her voice tentative and slightly trembling.

"Yes, come in—and shut the door," he mumbled.

She entered the room, standing near the wall farthest away from his desk. Hands behind his head, he sat back in his chair, slowly eyeing her up and down, from head to toe. "In my twenty years of coaching, I've never seen a team play as badly as this one. And you. I've given you so many chances. You missed everything that came your way today. You have a place on this team because of me. You know that, don't you?" He leaned forward, getting up and stepping toward her. He was confronting her now, his hand against the wall just over her shoulder, his face squarely in front of hers. "I expect more of you. I want more of you. You owe me that." He moved his right hand down onto her shoulder, then abruptly over her left breast, pinning her against the wall. "Do you get what I mean? Do you?"

She gasped, trying to move her face away from his. Grabbing her chin, he held her in his gaze. "Don't screw this up. You have a lot at stake." With that, he kissed her hard, parting her lips and forcing his tongue into her mouth.

Instinctively, she pulled away, trying to slide toward the door. "You liked it well enough when I made things go your way," he growled. "Just don't forget who's in charge here."

Quickly, Annie nodded and fled out the door. She needed to breathe.

3

One week before the coach's death

It had been a dismal day. They were playing in a nonconference tournament in Illinois, something they did every year to get practice before their conference season started. While their team was ranked first in their division, they had stumbled in the last game, losing by more than ten points. "A fricking circus," Coach had screamed at them. He had really chewed them out for the loss, calling attention to how each one of them had screwed up. Demoralized, they were ashamed of how they had done. Pegged as the strongest team in the school's history, the outcome brought their record to 0-3, not the leadership position their coach—or they—had expected or wanted. After the fans left the arena, he made them run fifty laps around the gym as a penalty for their poor performance. Exhausted and beaten down, they retreated to their hotel, finding their way to their captain's room.

"I hate him," Juanita said. At 5'2", she was quick and energetic, usually the first to intercept the ball. "He really laid into me during the first timeout. Called me a lazy slug. I couldn't stop a couple of kills, but I'm betting no one in this division could have done any better. I don't want to play for him anymore," she said.

One of the freshmen piped up, "I know. When he was recruiting, he was so positive and told me how he always supported his players whether they were winning or losing. He pulled me when I made one mistake. I didn't get to play the rest of the match. I hate sitting on the sideline. And I'm scared he's going to pull me from the team. I would lose my scholarship, and I can't stay here without that."

"Sorry," Annie said. "He put me in for you, Madison, and I couldn't do anything right. It was really awkward. I know I didn't do well for you guys. I wish I could have done better."

Madison sulked quietly, fidgeting with a piece of fuzz on the bedspread.

"Well, he never let me play at all," one of the freshmen complained. "I never got in the game. I had three schools recruiting me, but I picked this one because of the promises Coach Pearson made. It really sucks."

The women continued their grumbling.

Finally, one of the women hushed everyone. "We should all just up and quit. He wouldn't have a job without us."

There was general murmuring of agreement until another spoke up, "But I WANT to play volleyball. I don't want to quit. Then I lose!"

Another said, "Plus, he'd figure something out. He'd pull up the JV team. We need to try something else. We need to get him fired."

"Really? How could we do that? What would we have to say happened? Coaches yell at teams all the time," Caitlin said in disbelief.

"His results have been too strong. His record is something like 201 wins to 47 losses. They would never let him go," Hanna, the team captain, said matter-of-factly. "It would be a waste of time. I can see the athletic director laughing in our faces and telling us to 'man up.'" She grimaced at the expression. "Our first few games have been miserable this year. He would accuse us of using the coach as a scapegoat."

There was a murmur of agreement.

"I know!" Caitlin piped up. "I have an idea. We're all great at bumping the ball. Let's bump HIM off." She laughed at her own joke. "We could make it look like an accident. Plus no one would guess we were behind it because we're all so wholesome and innocent," she said, fluttering her eyelashes, trying to make herself look the part.

Brooke punched Caitlin in the arm. "Speak for yourself," she teased her.

"*Okay, you're so smart. How would we do it?*" *one of the sopho-mores asked.*

"*We could each play our own part, so it isn't on any one of us,*" *Caitlin continued.* "*Brooke, you could loosen the bolt at the right side of the ref's stand that he leans on. Juanita, you could loosen the left side. Hanna, you could loosen the bolts on the top step. Madison and Annie, you could each untighten the bolts on the other rungs of the ladder. My boyfriend does the scoreboard for the athletic department. Maybe he could arrange for something to fall from the ceiling.*" *She laughed at the thought of it.* "*I can see the headline now, 'Coach dies in the net.' It would serve him right for how he treats us.*"

All the players burst into laughter. The thought of knocking off their coach had lightened their mood, which had been very somber. "*Ah, in our dreams,*" *Brooke sighed. They all nodded and went off to the hotel rooms they shared.*

4

Tuesday after the Coach's death

As Carley drove to the campus from her lake home, a forty-five-minute drive lined with lakes and ponds, then farmland, she was inundated with feelings of nostalgia. Her mind bounced from thought to thought.

College had been such a great time in her life. She loved volleyball, not just for the sport, but because of how it stretched her confidence as a leader. They'd had so much success as a team. She had come into her own there—physically on top of her game, with a lot of friends, focused on a career in marketing that had great promise. Her future had seemed so exciting. What a contrast that was to what she felt now. She still wasn't over her father's death. Not knowing he had been murdered until two years later was still hard to comprehend. That he had been killed for his patents had fooled everyone. She should have known better. The doctors thought he had a heart attack. But he was in such good shape. And he was young. Shouldn't someone have been suspicious?

Her mind shifted to what she'd left behind in Minneapolis. How she missed her friends and co-workers. When her company moved to New York, it was great she was offered a six-month consulting contract. But that safety net would be up in three months. What was she going to do then?

And she thought about Mac. How he had deceived her. How she had to move out of the condo they shared. How alone she felt now. How stupid she had been. Luckily, she had the cabin at Pelican Lake from her father, so at least she had a place to live. She felt both grateful to be back in a place that meant so much to her, and humble, because life had definitely handed her several lemons. She shook her head as if to brush off the bewilderment she felt.

Entering the main entrance gate to campus, she felt a wave of familiarity sweep over her. Blue and gold banners flew over the quad. The campus gardens were in full bloom with vibrant shades of fall—oranges, reds, yellows. Walking in pairs or trios, students were chatting, laughing, happy to be back in their own world. The sprawling acres and red brick buildings made her feel right at home. While she had been on campus for an alum/senior volleyball game the previous spring, she hadn't returned often in the twelve years since she graduated. As a student, her volleyball team had taken second in the nation, falling in the final match to a superior team from California. And, as captain, she felt great pride in the teamwork they had and all they had accomplished. They had worked and played hard together, and it had paid off. In the end, they couldn't overcome the strength of their final opponent. But what a run they'd had, the best the school had ever seen. She imagined the team must feel pretty devastated now, having lost their coach. Her coach, his predecessor, had been her inspiration and mentor. It would be an honor to have the chance to be that for the players. However, she'd never coached. A little voice inside her wondered if she could deliver what the athletic director—and the team—needed now.

As she walked into the slightly dank, darkly lit gym, she was greeted by a familiar face. Vic, the janitor, was sweeping the floor with the same cleaning compound that always made her sneeze. Spotting Carley, Vic waved and called to her, "Hey there, Missy!! What are you doing around here?"

He used to help her set up equipment for captain's practices. Vic was hard working, dependable, and a little slow, with a heart of gold. Having worked for the athletic department for more than thirty years, he was known and beloved by students. "We've had a lot going on here the past two days," he said forlornly.

She realized Vic was probably the one who had found the coach. "I bet it's been pretty tough on you," she said. Looking up, she spotted the hole in the ceiling where the scoreboard had been attached. It made her shiver.

Vic nodded. "It was a real shock to everyone." Pointing the direction to the athletic director's office, he added, "I bet you're headed that way. There's been a lot of activity here these past couple of days."

Carley nodded and gave him a quick hug before she headed toward the office. Brad Anderson, the athletic director, was meeting with a young man. "Come on in, Carley. We were just wrapping up." With that he gave a nod to his visitor, who grabbed his laptop and left.

"The editor of our school paper," he noted. "He was here to get details for the story he's writing about Coach Pearson. The campus is pretty much abuzz."

"I'm sure it's quite a shock to students," Carley said. "And to you, too. I read the article in the paper this morning. How ironic that he died in the volleyball net. It had to be a pretty weird confluence of circumstances that made that happen."

"That's what the medical examiner seemed to think as well," Brad said seriously. "They're running an autopsy. Maybe they'll find he had a heart condition or some other medical condition that contributed to his fall. So far, it looks like a concussion and a broken neck. Certainly, the scoreboard would have made a lot of racket on its way down. It was pretty shocking." He paused. "Did you know him?"

Carley said, "I only met him briefly at the annual alum/senior game last spring." *And I wasn't impressed,* she thought to herself.

She found him somewhat rude and overbearing. At 6'2", he had a definite height advantage over her. His blonde, spiky hair gave him a look of cool confidence. He had a tight, athletic body and was wearing spandex shorts when she'd seen him, always an odd look for a grown man. "I didn't know him well," she added.

"I could really use your help now. I heard you were back in the area. I don't know if you're staying long, but I wondered if you could take over coaching the team. It's hard to imagine going on, but for the players, it seems pretty important. We'd pay you, of course. We have that money in our budget. There are five practices and two games a week, Tuesday or Wednesday evenings and Friday evenings or Saturday during the day, most of which will be out of town. There will only be a couple of games here, and some of those won't be standard conference games."

"You're in luck. Right now, I have a consulting contract for a few more months. My former employer moved their headquarters to New York. I didn't want to move, and I was lucky they offered me a six-month contract. I design marketing programs for new product launches. I've been working remotely and have a lot of freedom to come and go. However, that contract is up in December. I've started job hunting in Fargo, but haven't found anything yet," she told him. "I'm planning on staying in the area. But what happens if I do find a job? Is there any flexibility with the schedule? What options might I have?"

"Let's cross that bridge when we come to it. I could get someone here to help out with some of the practices, but I'd need your leadership for the games."

"How are the players doing?" Carley asked. "This has to be quite a jolt."

"It has been," he said, shaking his head and glancing around his disheveled office. "Quite a tragedy. We're all struggling here. I called the team together the day it happened, and they were reeling from the news. One of them threw up. All of them were pretty distraught. No one has stopped by since then. That was

three days ago; maybe they're doing better now." He paused, toy-
ing with the pencil on his desk, abruptly setting it down. "When
could you start?"

"Probably tomorrow. Right now, the project I'm working on
only takes about four to five hours a day, and I have a fair amount
of flexibility."

"Great. Let's do it," he said, rising to shake her hand. "I'll
email a contract to you tonight, along with a little information
about the players, and you can meet the team tomorrow afternoon.
They start at 4:00. Okay?"

As she rose and shook his hand, Carley wondered what she
was getting herself into.

5

Friday night before the coach dies

It was the second game of the season, and the women were nervous. The coach had threatened to cancel the season if they didn't do better than they had in the first game. Hanna was, of course, setting, and Brooke, Caitlin and Juanita were in as expected. Annie, the only freshman in the starting lineup, was taking Madison's place. Everyone felt edgy, stomachs in knots, trying hard not to let it show.

The score in the first game was now 17–5, not in their favor. Hanna had set the ball to Caitlin, who missed it altogether. The coach pulled Caitlin immediately, putting a freshman in her place. As she walked by him, he said in a loud stage-whisper to her, "You're a fucking screw up."

While Caitlin wasn't particularly intimidated by the coach, his profanity startled her. She watched her boyfriend in the nearby stands leap to his feet, shouting at the coach to go f--- himself. She didn't want the shouting match to get out of control. Looking the coach directly in the eye, she said, "People are watching. If I were you, I'd think twice about saying something like that out loud, in front of the fans."

The coach did a double take and said, "Go sit down. I don't want to hear anything more out of you." Of course, she knew she would be sidelined for the rest of the game.

After a while, the coach substituted Madison for Annie. But it wasn't long before he pulled her and put Annie back in.

"What the hell are YOU doing?" Coach snarled at Madison on the sideline. "You can't do anything right. Maybe you can learn something from Annie."

Madison could feel her face flushing from the neck up, her red-headed complexion making it obvious when she was upset. As she stood on the sidelines holding a clipboard and tracking her teammates' stats, she could feel venom rising in her stomach. Others had made bigger mistakes, and he hadn't pulled them. Her parents had come all the way from Mandan, no small trek, to watch her. Her boyfriend was in the stands. She could feel their concern for her, which made it worse. It was hard to be sidelined when all she wanted to do was play.

The coach hadn't always been so curt with her, she remembered. When she had started as a freshman two years ago, she was one of his favorites, which pissed off some of her teammates. She didn't mind. She was a strong player, and she liked having his attention. That ended when Annie, the new freshman, came along. They were both outside hitters, both stars in high school, both heavily recruited by other schools. She thought she'd made the right choice, but now she wasn't so sure. And Annie, with her quiet, demure way, her blonde hair and blue eyes, made her even more self-conscious of her out-of-control, frizzy red hair.

She knew she'd made a mistake with Coach. After they'd win a game, he'd come and find her on the bus, sing out a loud song to her, and mess up her hair. It wasn't awful; it just felt weird. And it was embarrassing. Other players mocked him behind his back. Finally, last year, she'd told him to knock it off. Now he did it with Annie. And now Annie was playing her position.

He wasn't going to put her back in the game, she was quite certain. As she stood miserably watching Annie miss several hits, time dragged on. No one seemed to notice her standing there.

After the match, which they lost in three consecutive sets, Madison rushed off to the locker room, not wanting to meet her parents' eyes with their look of consolation. Tears of humiliation stung her eyes. She just wanted to get out of there.

An hour later as she was leaving the locker room, she trudged through the now-empty gym. Her throat was raw, her whole face hurt, her stomach was clenched from stress and anger. She thought about the conversation the team had had in the hotel in Illinois. She didn't really want the coach dead; she just wanted to get even. Approaching the ref's stand, she pulled a securing pin from the top step. Wrapping her hand around the pin, she slipped her fist into her jacket pocket. It gave her a sense of satisfaction, knowing she'd done it. It wouldn't hurt anyone. No one else would do their part. It just made her feel slightly vindicated.

6

Carley and Brad stood in front of the team, twelve young women seated cross-legged in a half-circle in the gym. Looking very morose, they stared at the floor or vacantly straight ahead. Brad began, "I know you have been through a lot this week. It's hard to lose a coach, especially under such difficult circumstances. However, we're going to keep playing. The university has decided not to cancel your season. Coach Pearson would want you to play. And for some of you, it's your last year. I don't want you to miss out. I've asked Carley Norgren, an alum, to coach the rest of the season, and she's agreed. Carley graduated twelve years ago and was part of the fierce team that made it to the national playoffs, ending up second in the nation. She's a great person, and I know you'll enjoy her energy and enthusiasm. Carley, why don't you tell the team a bit about yourself?"

"Thanks, Brad," Carley said, stepping forward into the circle. She stooped and picked up a volleyball on the edge of the circle, balancing it in one hand. "Volleyball is still my passion. I'm a setter and have played in a co-ed adult league in the Cities since college. I've been thinking about finding a group in Fargo. I live at my lake home on Pelican Lake now and work part-time on a contract basis, so I have enough flexibility to make this work. I'm really looking forward to getting to know each one of you and figuring out how I can help. I hear you have a lot of talent, and my goal is to help you develop that. How about telling me a little about yourself? Tell me something fun I couldn't find out about you unless you told me—like a hobby or a special accomplishment. Hanna, let's start with you." She tossed the ball to her. Carley intentionally started with the one who was clearly the leader of the team. At 5'8', Hanna wasn't the tallest, but she was darling, blonde, and exuded energy. Carley blushed when she realized how much Hanna resembled her, only Carley's hair was shorter now, and she was thirty-four, not twenty-one.

"Well, I guess you already know my name. I'm Hanna. I'm a senior and the team captain. The position I play is setter. I'm guessing you already knew that, too. I'm from Alexandria, Minnesota. My biggest claim to fame is that every year I participate in the county fair. When I was 9, I was 'Miss Douglas County Fair Princess.' I've won blue ribbons in dance and crafts at the fair. Last summer, I won the lawn mowing derby. I was the only girl who entered the contest. So I guess you could say I'm a little competitive."

The young woman next to her spoke up, and Hannah flipped the ball to her. "A LITTLE competitive!! Ha!! I've known you for three years, and you're the most competitive person I know," Brooke laughed. "Hi, I'm Brooke, also a senior and it's my job to smack the ball. Hanna and I have been roommates since we were sophomores, so we know each other pretty well. I'm from Williston, home of the oil boom. I grew up on a farm that's an oilfield now. I have almost no other talent than volleyball. Seriously. My nickname in high school was 'Bean.' Or 'Beanpole.' Or sometimes just 'Pole.' Or 'Stretch.' Or 'Tree.' I'm sure there were a few others."

Carley knew from his notes that Coach Pearson had his own nickname for her, which she wouldn't repeat. At 6'2" and with short, dark hair, Brooke was the "tallest tree" on the team. She was lean, but slow. At her height, it was hard to get her feet to leave the ground. Luckily, she had good aim and a wicked kill shot. *Brooke and Hanna couldn't be more opposite, at least in appearance, but they have the makings of a dynamic duo,* Carley mused. Brooke bounce-passed the ball to her left.

The redhead to her left was next. "Hi, I'm Madison. I'm a junior from Mandan, about three hours from here. Mandan is 'where the West begins.' Or, at least, that's our city slogan. I own a pair of red cowboy boots that are my favorite possession, and I wear them everywhere." *To go with her flaming red hair,* Carley thought to herself. Madison glanced at the girl to her left, tossing her the ball.

"I'm Juanita, a junior," she said, "I'm from Bismarck, and I used to play against Madison. Our two schools were strong rivals. You've heard of Bismarck-Mandan, right? We were on the same traveling team outside of the regular school season. My claim to fame is I love to bake. My best dessert is butter pecan pie. Mmmmm." The rest of the team groaned at the thought of her delicious butter pecan pie. *At 5'2, she would probably be even quicker if she didn't enjoy her own baking quite so much,* Carley chuckled silently.

Carley turned to Annie, "Okay, you're next." She gestured, and Juanita flipped the ball to her.

Annie stammered, "I'm a freshman and I'm from Detroit Lakes. I don't know. I don't have much to say. I'm just glad to have a chance to play."

Caitlin piped up, "What she isn't telling you is that she was the Coach's new pet. He picked a new freshman pet every year. Everyone else was toast. Except for her. 'Have you seen how Annie can hit the ball? Did you see Annie get under that spike? Did you watch Annie block that player? Annie this, Annie that. You're lucky you're so sweet, Annie, or we'd all hate you!" Caitlin kidded her.

Annie blushed and shoved the ball toward Caitlin, who missed it on purpose. As the feisty one of the group, Caitlin delighted in stirring the pot. "I'm from the Twin Cities. Who knows why I decided to come to this god-forsaken place," she said, rolling her eyes. "Actually, I came for love. My boyfriend is a senior at the university, majoring in engineering. Outside of volleyball, I've loved it here. Great people. Fairly interesting classes. Volleyball has been kind of miserable. But this team isn't going anywhere anyway. So, I'm just making do."

Carley blinked at her honesty. "Well, we're going to do more than just make do. You all have the skill. We just have to get your rhythm going."

They continued until everyone had had a chance to say something. There weren't many more surprises. They were a good bunch, Carley concluded. She hoped they could start loosening things up.

Of course, she already knew their stats and had a pretty good sense of what positions they played and how well they played them. No one displayed much emotion or enthusiasm. "Let's get started with some warm-ups and a little scrimmage so I can see what you've got," Carley suggested.

The young women slowly got up and stretched. No one said much to Carley or each other. Brad looked at Carley and asked, "You good? I have to return a call from a major donor who wants to know what's going on."

Carley gave him two thumbs up, though she wasn't certain the team was off to a good start yet. Brad headed back to his office, leaving her in charge.

None of the players seemed to have much energy. Peppering balls to each other, they half-heartedly swatted the returns. "Glum" was the word that came to Carley.

Calling the team back together after fifteen minutes of watching their low energy, she said, "Hmmm. Doesn't feel like you're really into this. What would help?"

Hanna suggested, "Could we call it a day? Come back and try again tomorrow? The coach's death has been pretty tough on all of us." The rest mumbled their agreement.

While her judgment told her it would be better if they pushed through their lethargy, Carley said, "Okay, on one condition. Tomorrow you come in with your game faces on."

Murmuring indicated to Carley they would, though, from the look in their eyes, she wasn't totally sure she believed them.

7

When her cell phone rang, Carley immediately recognized the caller ID. She answered with more cheerfulness than she felt. "Hi, Jeff! How are you doing?"

"I've had a busy week. I closed on two houses, so I'm feeling pretty flush. I wondered if you'd like to grab a bite to eat and a movie Saturday night. I don't know what's playing, but I'm sure we can figure something out. I thought you could use some fun about now."

Sitting at her cabin's kitchen table, shuffling through her mail, Carley felt torn. She didn't have anything going on over the weekend outside of volleyball, but she also didn't want to have Jeff depend on her for anything other than an occasional outing. *He's a nice guy,* Carley thought to herself. *Nice, but a little dull. And we have no future together. No spark there. None.* While she appreciated the fun, light things they had done together over the last couple of months, she was quite certain he was hoping for more than she felt. He had been a good diversion, but that was it. She needed that when she was first at the lake and knew no one. She didn't mind going out with someone just for the fun of it—dancing, movies, WE Fest country rock concerts. But now it was reaching the point relationships eventually hit when it was time to decide about moving forward. He had started talking about taking a vacation together. That didn't interest her in the least. At the same time, she didn't want to hurt his feelings. He didn't deserve that, either. He was a really nice guy, after all.

"I don't think so. I've started coaching a college women's volleyball team, and we have a game on Saturday. Most likely I'll be too tired after that." She doodled absentmindedly on a scratch pad.

"Oh—did you take over for that coach who died? That was pretty freaky. How's the team doing?"

"The players were traumatized by the whole thing. Eventually, I hope they'll get over it, but probably not this season."

"Well, if you change your mind, let me know. I'd love to do something with you," Jeff said.

"Will do. And congratulations on selling two houses in one week!" She was going to have to be more direct, which she dreaded. *Maybe he'll get the hint if I turn him down a couple more times,* she thought to herself. After saying goodbye, she set the phone on the counter, and sighed.

In front of her was the Fargo morning paper detailing what happened at her lake home over the summer. The headline read, "Former Professor on Trial for Drugs and Embezzlement." The article described in detail how James Reston, aka Gordon Locklear, a former colleague of her father on the chemistry faculty at State, had orchestrated revenge for his firing. Not only had he stolen the rights to her father's patent, he formed a group of investors to manufacture his spectrometer. Worst of all, he had disguised her father's death as a heart attack. The writer described Reston as "a brilliant mastermind devoid of ethics." She could agree with that. And she had fallen for him. Of course, he had a great story about how close he had been to her father that sucked her right in. She shuddered at her naïveté, how vulnerable she had been, how narrowly she escaped his grasp. The only good thing to come from it was her friendship with Mark, who had literally saved her life. She shook her head, wishing she could evade the notoriety the case was bringing.

Wanting a distraction, Carley took out Abigail Rose's leash, much to the dog's great excitement. She hadn't been exercising her since she'd been away from home this week. "Come on, Girl. Let's go."

As Abigail Rose sniffed her way down the road lined with trees in different shades of gold, yellow, red, and green, Carley was glad to see someone else out for a walk. Ambling up the road with her small dog in tow was a neighbor who had been a close friend of her mother. "Well, hi there, Hon! How are you doing these days? Has life started settling down for you yet?"

"Yes, I think it finally has," Carley said, smiling. Since Betty Sue lived only four homes down from her, Carley was quite sure she had witnessed the chaos of the summer and read the morning paper. They stood together while the dogs nosed about. "Things are a bit calmer now than they were a few weeks ago. I imagine I was the talk of the beach."

"Well, life is pretty dull around here. It's not every day we have the FBI, a drug ring, and a bad business plot all revolving around one cottage. Plus a burned down garage. I bet it was pretty exciting for you, too," Betty Sue remarked.

"Not exactly what I planned when I came up here," Carley said. "I was more surprised than anyone."

"I was very sorry to learn about your father. He was such a great man; he didn't deserve to die because of someone's greed."

"I know," Carley said, looking at the ground. Not wanting the conversation to become too heavy, she said, "Say, aren't you involved with State? I'm the new coach for their women's volleyball team. You probably heard about what happened to Coach Pearson."

"Oh my gosh, I did. That was terrible. And a little ironic. A volleyball coach found hung up in the volleyball net. Well, good for you. I'm an alum and I contribute there, so I hear a lot about what's going on. I was never into sports, though, and I admire you."

She paused. "Say, I've been meaning to call you. I'm part of a book group that has women of all ages in it—your age to mine. Well, almost your age. And now that fall has arrived, some of our members are heading south for the winter. Would you have any interest in joining? We have a couple more meetings before people leave for the winter. The next meeting is Tuesday at my home. I provide chicken and lettuce, and everyone else brings fixings for a salad. You could bring whatever you want. Our group is called the 'You Don't Have to Read the Book Book Club.' So don't worry if that isn't enough time to read the book!"

Carley laughed. It was just her kind of group. She was dying to meet some women at the lake. Over the summer she had met a lot of men, but not many women, and she had always counted on female friends to get through life. "Thank you. I would love to join! Let me know the name of the book you're reading, and I'll at least try to skim it. We'll have some time to kill on the team bus on Monday, and that will give me time to read." Giving each other a quick hug, they tugged their dogs away from each other and headed their respective ways. Carley smiled as she continued down the road.

Carley was having a hard time getting her feet under her. She missed the constancy of a steady boyfriend like Mac. She had stopped missing him. But having someone serious in her life made it easier to have fun things to do, especially spur of the moment. She thought she'd found "the one" in Gordon over the summer, but she was wildly wrong about that. Uncharacteristically, she had let her guard down fast. She knew now she'd be much better off taking a break from men altogether. She could feel her smile fading as she walked.

The man three doors down rested his binoculars in his lap. He thought she looked sad. Maybe she needed some cheering up. Maybe he should make his move soon. For now, he'd just keep watching. He picked the binoculars up again and watched Carley until she disappeared into her cabin.

8

"How's the team doing?" Mark asked Carley as they sat down at the Mexican restaurant on the northwest shore of Pelican Lake. It was a rough, hole-in-the-wall, casual kind of place. With so many residents on Pelican Lake and so few restaurants, it was usually hopping.

"Not as well as I hoped," Carley replied. "The coach's death has really sent them into a tailspin. It's only been three days since I started working with them, but they're out of sync with each other. Our first game together is this Wednesday in the Cities. I'm not holding my breath that they'll win. It will be the first time I've been back there in three months, and I'm hoping a close friend of mine will show up."

"I'm sure it's not your coaching. I hope you don't take it personally. You said they have a lot of skill. Maybe they'll snap out of it when the pressure is on." He paused. "Will you try to see Mac while you're there?"

Carley was startled by his question. She forgot he knew about Mac, her former lover, roommate, and almost-fiancé. "No, I don't intend to see Mac. Not ever, if I can help it." She pushed on, "And I hope the team gets with it, or my debut as a new coach will be pretty dismal. Not that I care about that. But I do care about these women. Hey, how's your cabin working out?" she asked, changing the subject.

"Not bad. I have an infestation of mice I'm working on right now. And I'm resealing windows that haven't had any attention for years. Exciting stuff, you know."

"How about work? Any interesting cases? Anything you can talk about?"

"No, nothing as exciting as blueprint machines and anhydrous ammonia," he said with a sly grin, gently referencing the events of the last summer.

Carley flushed. "Don't remind me. It's going to take me years to get over those four words." She paused. "I have some interesting news. I got an email yesterday from a man who competed with Manufacturek, the company that was illegally distributing a version of my father's spectrometer. He wants to meet. He indicated he'd like to explore a licensing agreement that would allow him to produce and distribute a spectrometer using my father's patent. He sounds legit—a chemical engineer, CEO of his company, which has about a hundred and twenty-five employees. I have a meeting with my patent attorney next week to discuss it."

Mark leaned forward. "Sounds interesting—potentially big. How will you know if what he's offering is reasonable? Do you know much about licensing? Or what the patents might be worth?"

"No, I know very little about any of that. The CFO of the company I work for now may be able to help me. He's a buddy. My company has several licensing agreements, and I know he has some experience, although not in this industry. I'll have to get my brother in the loop, too, because we own my father's patents jointly. I'm not sure his PhD in English Lit will help us much here, but he has contacts where he lives in L.A. who might be able to help. If you have any ideas, cough 'em up."

"I don't know much about corporate finance. I know a couple of entrepreneurs in Fargo, though. Maybe they could help you. I hope you get some good advice." Pausing, he said, "I have something I want to ask you about, totally unrelated to spectrometers. Do you see the poster on that wall?" He pointed to a flyer adjacent to them. "There's a beach volleyball competition at the hotel near Lake Melissa this Saturday. Why don't you enter it?"

"I've heard about that. I haven't played beach volleyball in a while. I'm really feeling out of shape," Carley said, sighing. "It looks like it's just bikinis with beer, but it's actually very intense."

"I'd come watch," Mark offered, with a sheepish grin.

"A good reason NOT to do it." She looked at him, rolling her eyes.

"Well, maybe we could go and watch if you decide not to enter it. That is, of course, if you don't have other exciting plans."

"I'll check my very, very busy schedule. Oh, what do you know? I'm free. This must be the last match of the season. September is getting pretty brisk for beach volleyball." She paused. "You know, some of the women on my team might be interested. Would you mind if I asked them?"

"Not at all. It could be fun," Mark responded.

Carley agreed. Outside of her occasional dates with Jeff, her social life was pretty quiet. Her summer fling with Gordon was enough complication to last for a long time. She and Mark had become good friends, but that was it. A good friend was exactly what she needed right now.

9

It was her first game as coach and Carley felt unexpected nerves kicking in as she walked along the bench next to the court. She was concerned for the young women. They had been quiet on the bus ride down to the Cities, and she was afraid a loss might make some of them decide to quit the team. *They have so much talent,* she thought to herself. She had seen recruiting tapes for several of them. They were rock stars in high school—captains, most valuable players, all-state athletes. She'd found game videos, too, though she hadn't looked at any of those yet. Volleyball had been such an important part of her life after college, and she didn't want to see them become so discouraged they would give it up. Trish, her best friend, had come to the game and was behind the bench a few rows up. Surprisingly, most of the parents of the players were a few rows up, too. Many of them had driven from great distances to be there. Carley was grateful for the support. She hoped the team would perform well, win or lose.

Bright lights, whistles blowing, the sound of volleyballs bouncing off the floor and walls as the two teams warmed up made the air in the gym electric. Their competitor was strong, one of the top three teams in the conference. Her team had fallen to seventh place with the most recent loss, but the season was still young. *They have the talent to be at the top,* she thought to herself. It was up to her to unleash that talent.

She had picked the starters based on seniority and track record. Hanna would set, Brooke would play middle, Juanita as libero—the designated back row player/best passer, Caitlin as defensive specialist, Madison as outside hitter, and Lauren, a freshman, as right side. She had promised all of them playing time and asked everyone to approach the game unselfishly. Her goal, she reiterated, was to get each girl playing at the top of her talent.

The ref blew his whistle to signal the start of the game. They won the coin toss. Hanna, the first to serve, hit the ball hard, but it shanked off to the left. Their competition aced the next six serves, with Carley's team scrambling to get to the ball. They weren't successful. As she watched, she was struck by how they seemed to lack confidence. Carley called a timeout. She looked each of the six in the eyes and said, "It's okay. You can do this. I know you can ace your serves. I've seen it in practice. I know you know how to pass the ball. Just take deep breaths and let your muscles do what they know how to do." The team pumped hands and went out on the court slightly more energetically than they had initially. It didn't matter, however. The momentum was with the other team.

The first set ended miserably, 25-7. Carley said, "Let's change things up a bit here." Keeping Hanna and Brooke in, she substituted four of the other starters. "I'll keep rotating everyone in until we find our rhythm. Deal?"

The team responded, "Deal."

Unfortunately, the second set was worse than the first one, with a final score of 25-4. Carley called the team together and said, "Here's the good news. You have nothing to lose. What you're doing now isn't working. Let's get your heads back in the game and just play your hardest. Don't worry about winning. Just worry about showing up." With that, she called up the rest of her freshmen.

Two freshmen, who hadn't been allowed to play in a game yet this season under Coach Pearson, high-fived each other. Nerves made them overreact at first, but soon they settled in and played moderately well. The opposition had their third string in, actually giving Carley's team a chance. And they took it. The score for the third set had State at 25 and the opposition at 18. Not bad. They'd take a win any way they could get it.

For the fourth set, the opposing team's coach put all the starters back in. While Carley stacked the deck with her strongest players, it wasn't enough, and they fell 25-15. Since matches like this were best-of-five, the team gathered up their jackets and bags and headed for the locker room.

On her way out of the gym, suddenly she was met by a big hug. "Trish!" In the excitement, Carley had almost forgotten her closest friend was at the game.

"That was ugly," Trish remarked with a straight face. "But you're up to it. Hope they're paying you enough."

Carley chuckled, "Hardly. But these are good players. It'll happen. Keep the faith."

"Oh, I will," Trish commented dryly. "You'd better, too. From what I can see, they need you. When can you come down here for a real visit? I miss you! And I need your help with my wedding plans."

Carley said, "My travel time will be pretty limited during the volleyball season. I'll be here for a few more games, but I have to go right back because we have practice the next day. November is probably my first chance for a longer trip. Let me know when you're free, and we'll figure something out. I miss you! And, yes, I want to find out how things are going with your very exotic destination wedding in the Dominican. February will be a perfect time for a get-away. I loved the picture of your dress. Wish I could have gone shopping with you," Carley said wistfully. "I miss my best friend."

"It's not the same without you here. Let me know when you get tired of living in the boonies and decide there's no place like home in Minneapolis. By the way, I think I've found your maid of honor dress. If you don't come back in November, you might get stuck with something you don't like," she said with a spark in her eye.

Carley wanted to tell her it was the groom she didn't like, but she had never dared say that out loud. Instead, she said, "Oh, you're going to blackmail me into coming? Yeah, that works. Love you, Kiddo. I'd better get going or the bus will leave without me." Carley gave Trish a big squeeze. "Thanks for coming." They were both a bit teary-eyed as they parted.

The four-hour bus ride back was quiet. Most of the young women were studying, with headsets plugged in. The two freshmen, having survived their first game, were the only ones chatting, giggling, almost giddy. They felt they'd finally had a chance to prove themselves, and they had done better than the starters. Carley asked Hanna, the captain, to come sit with her for a while. "Where do we go from here? What advice do you have for me?" she asked.

Hanna thought for a minute. "You're very calm. That's good. And you don't yell at any of us like Coach Pearson did. I think we just need more time. Don't be too soft on us next week, though. We have to prove we're tougher than this."

Carley nodded in agreement. "Thanks, Hanna. That's good input. I like your leadership style. I need you to talk with each girl and reassure her. Give your teammates a pep talk. I've been a captain, too. Your role can make a big difference here."

As Hanna went back to her seat, Carley sighed heavily and pulled out the playbook to think about how she could coach each girl. She wasn't at all sure that was where the answers lay. Or even what the questions were.

10

When she returned home late that evening, she was glad to see her dog, Abigail Rose, and her cockatiel, Prattle, who didn't seem particularly distressed by how long she'd been gone. Mark had come over to let Abigail out and feed her. She had fed Prattle in the morning, and the bird was now resting comfortably, standing on one foot with her other foot tucked well under her wing. Probably the hardest thing about this coaching job was leaving her pets when she had out-of-town games. And more than half of their games were out of town, usually at a fair distance.

It was a relief to be home with the warmth and coziness of her cabin surrounding her. How she loved the stone fireplace, the cozy braided rug that lay in front of it, and the almost-antique, overstuffed chairs that made the living room very inviting. The cabin's rustic spirit was soothing to her. In spite of all that had happened over the summer, she felt safe here. Go figure. It was as if the worst had already happened. *That's probably a false sense of security,* she thought to herself.

Although it was after midnight, she was too churned up to go to sleep just yet. Pouring herself a glass of red wine, she grabbed one of the earlier game videos out of her briefcase and put it in her DVD player. The match was the first of the season, and the team seemed to be playing well. As setter, Hanna had control of the court. Brooke's kills as middle were strong and well-aimed. Brooke was slamming balls into the back corner of the opponents' court where they couldn't get to them. Juanita was a hotshot little libero, popping up the ball no matter how hard it came flying over the net. They looked confident, strong, not at all like the team she had just watched play in real life.

In the next play, Hanna set the ball to Brooke; it wasn't the best set, but it wasn't a bad one, either. Brooke missed it, swinging emptily at the air in front of her. Coach Pearson immediately swapped out Brooke, got Brooke on the sidelines, and screamed at her, standing about two inches from her face. She could see Brooke jerk back from the spit hitting her as he yelled. Red-faced, she went to stand on the sidelines with the others. *Ouch*, Carley thought. She wondered if the coach would put Brooke back in. She was a great player.

Their team was ahead 12-7. The coach called a timeout to go over strategy. He stood with his arm around Annie's shoulder. That surprised Carley. Most coaches knew better than to physically touch a player. When they were done, he patted her on the shoulder, making direct eye contact with her. It was almost suggestive. Annie blushed and went back out on the court, seeming to shake it off. *What was that?* Carley wondered to herself. Perhaps the coach needed a refresher on how to deal with women on the court. She wondered if he'd been taken to task for that behavior.

The coach acted the same throughout the rest of the game. He never forgave mistakes, except those of Hanna and Annie. Players were pulled the minute they did something wrong and, from the look of it, chewed out pretty energetically. He didn't put Brooke in after he pulled her. Four of the team members never played, even though the team won all three sets pretty handily. The scores in the final game were much closer than in the first two, and the players looked a little more on edge. She could understand why. Yet this coach got results, had a winning record, had received coaching awards in the conference. She'd never treat the team like that. But she needed to light a fire under them. There needed to be a healthy balance between being yelled at and being pampered; neither extreme was productive for the team. Exhausted, she decided it was time to call it a night, turned off the DVD player and the lights, and headed upstairs to bed, feeling a little discouraged by how much ground the team had lost.

Meanwhile, the man three cottages down watched through his binoculars until the lights went out in her cabin. He would sleep better now, knowing that she was where she belonged.

II

By noon, Carley had reviewed the other three game videos at her office and had pulled together some thoughts for each girl. Practice was still about half an hour off when there was a knock at her office door in the gym. It was Vic. "Hi there, Missy. How goes the battle?"

"Oh, I've had better weeks. What's up with you, Vic?"

"Well, I just wanted to brighten up your day." Pulling out a framed photo of the Red River, Vic said, "I'm a wannabe photographer. I took a bunch of photos twenty years ago. My wife and I used to walk along the river together when she was still alive. It was peaceful on those banks. This is my favorite spot. Hope it will bring you a little peace when you look at it. In the meantime, you keep up the good work." He offered it to her.

Studying it, she smiled. "Thanks, Vic. It's beautiful. I remember this spot from my days as a student here. How thoughtful of you. I'll smile every time I look at this photo. It'll help me relax."

"You need to stay relaxed. You're a breath of fresh air, and we all want to keep you happy. You're good for these girls. Well, I'd better get back to work. You take care now."

Carley gave Vic a big smile. "Thanks, Vic. This is very touching. And my office needed a little brightening up."

Shortly after Vic left, there was another knock on the door.

"Hi Annie! Come on in." She put down what she was reviewing and motioned to Annie to have a seat on the opposite side of her desk. "What's up?"

"I just came by to tell you I'm dropping the team. It's just too hard since Coach's death. And I have a really tough load of classes this semester." Annie sputtered, "I don't want to play anymore."

Carley leaned forward. "I don't believe you," she said, looking Annie squarely in the eyes. "I don't believe you don't want to play anymore. I know it's been a hard time. But I don't want you to give up. I'm asking you to give me a chance. And give yourself a chance to move beyond all that's happened. I watched you play in the third game, and I know you have talent. Coach Pearson hadn't tapped into that. I'm sure it's been a discouraging fall. Please, don't quit now."

Annie looked uneasy. "There's more to it," she said. "The girls…I don't know," she stammered. Pausing, she seemed hesitant to continue.

"Everyone needs to settle down. I'll work hard on teamwork and trust," Carley said. "You're a good person and a good player. And you deserve to be on a good team. Let's see what we can do about that."

Annie nodded tentatively, paused as if she were going to say more, then backed out of the office, heading slowly to practice.

Whew, Carley thought to herself. *I'm not sure I convinced her. She's the first one to cave. How many more will be on her heels? How do I keep a mass exodus from happening?* She didn't want the school's volleyball program to end on her watch.

Closing her laptop, she picked up the notes she'd just printed for each girl. She planned to meet with each one to build a relationship and a plan. She hoped that would work. Her first order of business was to work on the lack of confidence she saw in all the players. They were so off-balance.

Awaiting her arrival in the gym, the young women stood in a circle, looking like the world was coming to an end. *Remember, it's just a game,* Carley coached herself. *No one is dying here.* When she realized the irony of what she was thinking, she winced. Quickly, she settled herself and, turning to the team, announced, "We're going to play a little game. I'm going to serve this volleyball to one of you. Your job is to bump it to another girl on the team. The next girl has to bump it to someone else. If you miss, you have to say what would help this team succeed." Without any further introduction, she aimed the ball at Hanna, who expertly dove to the ground and passed the ball to Brooke. Brooke bumped the ball to Caitlin, who bumped it to Madison. Madison wasn't quite as lucky as the others. She got under the ball, but it went flying out of the now enlarged circle.

"Okay, Madison. What would help this team be better?"

"We need to have more fun. It's always so serious. That's not why any of us are in this sport. We're here because we love to play. Okay, and for our scholarships. But let us play, and let us have fun playing," Madison said.

"Good. Now serve the ball to someone else," Carley directed her.

Madison spiked the ball to Juanita, who, as the libero, was used to quick turn-arounds. She expertly got under the ball and bumped it a little off target to Hanna, who couldn't get to the ball in time.

"Okay, Hanna. You go," Carley said.

"We have to take responsibility for ourselves. We've been playing like shit. Let's own up to that and move on. We're much better than we've been playing."

"Good. Thanks, Hanna. Now it's your turn to pass the ball."

Hanna shot the ball to Annie, who missed. Looking embarrassed, Annie said, "We can't have secrets."

Puzzled, Carley said, "Do you feel the team has secrets now?"

"It's possible," Annie admitted. The rest of the team shot her glances.

"I hope when the time is right you can share those secrets with me," Carley said. "Your turn, Annie. Serve the ball."

Annie served it successfully to Brooke, who grabbed the ball. "I want a chance to say something. Everyone here needs to get

beyond Coach Pearson's death. We're big girls. No more moping."
The team nodded in agreement.

Carley wasn't at all sure they were ready to do that. And what did Annie mean about "secrets?"

12

Mark offered to pick her up for the beach volleyball tournament at the hotel on Lake Sallie. It wasn't really a hotel, though it had been at one time. Now it was a restaurant, bar, and general hang-out area. Carley had invited team members to come and play, though she made them promise no one would sprain an ankle. The deadline to enter the tournament was Wednesday, and she knew four from her team had signed up—Hanna, Brooke, Madison, and Caitlin.

As Mark pulled into her driveway, Carley realized how much this might look like a date to the women—or to Mark. However, after two minutes in the car, any concern she had about Mark disappeared. They bantered as they always did. "Beach volleyball might be one of my favorite sports," Mark said in a very under-stated way.

"What's not to love about it?" Carley laughed. "Women in bikinis, a lot of action, and beer."

"I know," Mark said. "It amazes me it's an Olympic sport." Carley punched him, not too gently, in the arm.

"Ow. You've got to stop doing that," he said in a kidding way. "Remember, I can have you arrested."

"Oh, you're a big talker." He was like a brother to her. Her own brother had moved to the other side of the country for his career, leaving a big void in her life. Mark filled that void. While she had been suspicious of Mark at first, she couldn't deny that they had become close friends. After all, he had uncovered that her father had been murdered. And he saved her after she had been kidnapped. Literally, he had saved her life. It had been great to have him nearby, and she thought it had been good for him, too.

"How did your game go last night?" Mark asked with interest.

Carley winced, "Not as bad as our game in the Twin Cities, but we didn't win. I'm glad to get these four women a little more competitive practice. It can't hurt—as long as no one sprains an ankle."

As they pulled up in the parking lot of the hotel, Carley said, "No leering at my players. You can ogle the competition instead."

Mark shot her a look as if to ask if she thought leering or ogling were really his style. He was pretty conservative, well-measured, well-groomed. With dark hair and glasses, at 5'10" with a sturdy build, he was good-looking in a nerdy, Clark Kent kind of way. Today he would be the only spectator in khakis, not jeans. Pretty buttoned-down, Carley thought to herself. She knew she didn't need to worry.

Immediately, they were greeted by Carley's foursome. They were drinking coffee, trying to wake up after a late Friday night game and party. It was brisk—only about fifty degrees—so all the players were wearing long-sleeved shirts and spandex instead of bikinis. She introduced them to Mark, who shook hands, addressing each by name. *I hope they're thinking he's too geeky for me,* Carley laughed to herself.

The six of them watched the first game, which was very energetic and evenly matched. Unlike college volleyball with six players on each side, this beach volleyball tournament, with only four players per side, was intense and quick. Each match was the best of two out of three games. The young women watched with interest. Only Caitlin had played beach volleyball before, and that was just for fun. Today the prize was $100 per player, a big incentive to win. For college students, that was a lot of cash.

They watched the next match all together. The State players weren't up for an hour and a half. Hanna and Brooke were explaining the finer points of the game to Mark, who listened appreciatively. Carley watched him out of the corner of her eye. They liked the male attention and were intrigued that he was an FBI agent.

Quite a crowd had gathered for the tournament, one of the last hurrahs of the summer. Everyone was pretty well bundled up, and it felt like fall was well underway. The women watched the other players intently. Suddenly, Madison elbowed Hanna. "Look over there."

The young women whispered and laughed among themselves. Finally, Carley's curiosity overcame her. "What's so funny?"

Brooke said, "Do you see that creepy looking guy over there?"

Carley studied the crowd intently, her eyes finally landing on a mid-fortyish bearded man in spandex shorts. The overall look wasn't becoming. "Him?" she nodded in the man's general direction.

"Yeah. He was a friend of our coach. He used to show up at practices every once in a while, and the two of them would go off and whisper. He came to some games, too. But Coach never introduced him to us, never told us who he was, never seemed completely comfortable when he was around. Do you think we should go up and talk with him?" Hanna asked the others.

"No way," Caitlin said emphatically. "He gives me the creeps. Men in spandex always have that effect on me. Do you think he plays volleyball?"

"At his height? Probably not," Madison said. "I wonder how he and Coach knew each other. I'm glad he won't be hanging around the campus anymore."

Mark was distracted by his phone, and Carley wondered if he was getting bored. She was relieved when it was time for their match. They were the strongest athletes on the State team and probably the best prepared for this level of competition. While beach volleyball seemed like a bar sport, it actually attracted some of the best athletes in the region.

Hanna's first set to Brooke was a success. Brooke slammed the ball between the two opponents. They high-fived each other. After gaining several points in a row, the other team rallied and, in the end, the foursome fell in the first game. During a timeout, Carley pointed out where the other women were positioned and where Brooke might have some success returning the ball. It worked. From that point on, the fierce college foursome outscored their opponents 21 to 16 in the second game, then 15 to 12 in the final set. Victorious, Hanna, Brooke, Madison, and Caitlin were whooping as they came off the court, stomach bumping each other, and giving high fives to near-by spectators. Because the tournament was single elimination, they only had one more match to play for the day and hoped to emerge victorious.

Carley thought she noticed the man watching the two intently after the match. Throwing back the last of his beer, he melted into the crowd, and Carley lost sight of him. Shrugging it off, she turned back to the young women, who were pulling off their long-sleeved shirts, as the day had warmed up. "Okay, what's your strategy for the grand finale?" Carley asked with a smile.

"Survival. We watched these four play earlier. They're good. I think one of them plays in a European league. I don't know if we stand a chance, but it would be great to get the $100 prize. I could get my car fixed," Brooke said.

"Just stay focused," Carley advised. "You can do this."

The first game was a tough one. Caitlin had a couple of spectacular digs while Madison had some equally impressive kills and some surprising blocks. Surprising, Carley thought, because the player on the other side of the net was two inches taller than Brooke, who was by far the tallest player on Carley's team. While the women nearly took the lead mid-game, they lost momentum toward the end, falling 21-18 to the other team. In the second game, looking slightly less centered, they quickly lost 21-12.

"Shoot," Brooke said as they came off the court. "I could have used that prize money," she moaned.

Carley thought to herself, *This has been the team issue all fall. Their confidence doesn't match their skill.*

"Madison, you had some great kill shots. Caitlin, you really got under the ball. You played such great defense. Well done!" Carley said. "And Hanna and Brooke, you were your usual dynamic duo."

"We lost and you're still trying to make us feel good," Caitlin bantered.

"You four looked great," Carley said. "And I know you haven't played much beach volleyball in the past. I'm proud of you."

Mark bought the young women large root beer sodas to celebrate, since they weren't allowed to drink during the season, especially not in front of their coach. It had been a fun day, and Carley was thankful Mark had come along.

In the car on the way back to the lake, Carley said, "Those four are talented players, but they have to learn how to win together as a team. Their confidence is weak. One of my big challenges is to get them to understand how talented they are and how to cooperate to win. I hope that can happen before the season ends."

"I trust you can, knowing you," Mark responded. "I watched you with those four. You have their confidence; they want to play well for you. That's half the battle coaching women."

Carley glanced his way, surprised by that comment. "How do you know about coaching women? You're absolutely right, but a lot of men, especially male coaches, don't get that. I know the one who died didn't."

"I coached a women's softball team in Fargo for a couple of years. I'll tell you more about it sometime."

"You're full of surprises," Carley remarked. "Oh, and what did you think about that friend of the coach? Didn't he look kind of creepy?"

"I got a picture of him on my phone. He looks familiar to me, which isn't a good sign. It probably means he has some drug ties. I thought I'd run him through a couple of my databases."

It pays to know the FBI, Carley thought to herself. Here she had thought he was bored and just playing with his phone. *He's good. Glad he's on my side.*

When Carley mentioned she thought he had been bored, he glanced at her sheepishly, "Remember, women, spandex, beer. Plus, four wonderful young women. And some time with you. Who could be bored?" He looked at her, smiling. "It would have been more fun if you had been playing. And I promise I wouldn't have ogled."

"You'd better not," she said, in a pretend threatening overtone. It had been a fun day. She had to admit they always had a good time together.

13

Carley wasn't sure how she could get the team's spirits back up. Hanna, Brooke, Caitlin, and Madison seemed energized by the beach volleyball they had played on Saturday. Sitting around before practice, Caitlin turned to Carley, "So who is Mark? Is he your boyfriend?"

"No, I told you he's just a friend. I had some trouble over the summer. He works for the FBI and had been working on part of the case that I was roped into. Anyway, some big things went down, and he saved me. We've been friends ever since."

"We know all about that. Brooke googled you after we met you the first time. We wanted to see your volleyball record. Instead, we read about everything that happened this summer at your place on Pelican Lake. Wow, that was intense!!! Don't you have a hard time staying there alone after all that happened?"

"I've got a dog and a bird who guard me pretty well. Plus, all the bad guys have been apprehended now."

"Tell us what it was like when you played in the national tournament. Was it the same level of volleyball we're playing?"

Carley laughed when she realized what they were getting at. They had no idea. Her team played against teams from California and Illinois that were twice as good as this team. *Sometime I'll show them the final game tape and impress them,* she decided. But not today. Today it might be demoralizing.

Carley's reverie was interrupted by the athletic director who took her aside. "We've just gotten word from the police who are investigating the death of the coach," he said quietly. "They're convinced his death wasn't an accident. Turns out the cables snapped after they'd been partially sawed through. They've changed the classification of the coach's death from 'accidental' to 'suspicious.'"

Carley gulped hard, trying to grasp what the athletic director was saying. The coach was murdered? That was hard to process. This was college sports, after all. Who would want to murder a volleyball coach? What should she tell the team? Should she tell them now? The athletic director added some details about the school's response, as she listened. She nodded, shook herself, and turned back to her team.

Not wanting them to hear the news around campus, Carley called the team together in a huddle. "I have some difficult news. The report from the initial investigation by the police has shown it's likely the coach was murdered. It appears the cables holding the scoreboard were sawed partially through, then snapped. They don't know anything more at this time, but I'm sure we'll hear about it as they do." She paused, deliberating. "We are continuing with the team as planned. In the meantime, don't come into the gym alone. Always make sure there are two or three of you together. We'll learn more as the week goes on. The coach's funeral has been postponed until they can complete the autopsy. They assume the only weapon was the scoreboard, but they will have to check that out as well. I'm so sorry. I know this is disturbing for you. But I promise the school and I will do everything in our power to keep you in the loop and safe. State is adding security staff to keep an eye on things. We don't have any reason to expect that anything further will happen. They are just being cautious."

The women looked like they had been socked in the stomach. *Not exactly the pick-me-up I was hoping for,* Carley thought to herself. "Let's call it a day. Do some extra pushups in your dorm room tonight, okay? And come back for the game tomorrow night rested. We can do this."

With that, the women put their hands in the middle of the circle and, calling "TEAM," began to disperse, wandering distractedly toward the locker room, exchanging alarmed glances, wide-eyed, silent.

14

She was happy to get home a little earlier than usual that evening. Scooping up Abigail Rose, she walked to the end of her dock, taking in the beautiful sunset. She had two Adirondack chairs on the dock platform, and she plunked down in one of them, mesmerized by the stillness of the water. It had been a crazy summer followed by a crazy fall. Would it ever let up? What would it take for her to feel settled in herself again? Her cell phone, buzzing in her pocket, interrupted her reverie.

"Hi there." It was Mark on the phone. "How is Week Two on the job?"

"Oh, geez," Carley replied. "I'm not sure what I've bitten off. The women are really out of sorts. It's like slogging in mud." She looked out at the lake, quiet at sunset.

"How about a distraction?"

"Sure. What do you have in mind?"

"Could I stop by?"

"Yes. I'm down on the dock."

About three minutes later, Mark appeared around the corner of the cabin, holding two beers. He walked down to the dock, and Carley motioned to him to sit down in the other Adirondack. "I've had a tough week, and I figured you might benefit from one of these, too."

He had read her mind. She said, "I love the distraction. Nothing good is happening on the court. Sometimes I think we're making progress, and the women are getting their act together. Then someone says something that puts them back in a funk. I'm surprised you're here at the lake tonight. What's going on with you?"

"I'm still working on the North Dakota drug trafficking case that involved our friend, Gordon. It has a lot of tentacles. One of our undercover agents went missing, and they found his body last night. It's sobering. No one is talking now, which is understandable. I know I'd hate to end up like that. So I'm out of the field for a couple of weeks. We're going to let things die down a bit. I want to spend more time here until the cold really hits." Pausing, he continued, "I've got some news for you. The coroner's report has come in on your coach. They've changed the ruling from accidental to suspicious. Maybe there's more to your volleyball coach than meets the eye."

"The athletic director told me before practice today. I had to tell the women. I still can't quite get my head around it. Who would kill a coach? After all, it's college volleyball we're talking about here. The lead detective on the case is going to meet with the team and me tomorrow to ask for our help in identifying anything suspicious. His name is Lieutenant Pete Collins. Do you know him?"

"He's a colleague of mine. We've worked on some cases together. Played racquetball once. He beat me."

"I'm surprised they've brought you in on a coach's death. Seems like that may be beneath your pay grade."

"No, I haven't been brought in on it at all," Mark answered. "That's not part of the FBI jurisdiction. We only get involved if something crosses state lines or has pretty massive implications. Nothing about the coach's death points to that right now, and the police are on it. We have a network of agencies that try to keep each other up to date on things that are out of the ordinary. And the coach's death is just that. They wanted to be sure we had it on our radar."

"Thanks. We'll meet with Collins tomorrow. I'm sure that will be interesting. You know, I'd appreciate it if some time you'd stop by with some good news!" She said, raising one eyebrow and grimacing slightly.

Mark chuckled, stood up, finished off his beer, gave her a quick eyeroll, and said, "I'll work on that."

15

Carley and the team were meeting with Lt. Collins that day. She knew she wouldn't be of much help to him. After all, she'd barely even met the coach. Certainly she hadn't murdered him to get his job, she laughed to herself. But she would do whatever the school asked her to do.

Collins knocked on the frame of her office doorway. "Lt. Collins," he announced. He was tall—about six feet, she figured, dark hair, about 45 years old with an air of authority. She introduced herself and explained she had just started coaching a week ago.

Very quickly it became apparent to the detective that Carley didn't have any knowledge of the coach, or the team, for that matter. He asked her to keep an eye out for anyone who might be suspicious, anyone who might have reason to dislike the coach, anyone who had a temper, anyone who might have been upset with the coach. A parent. A boyfriend. A player.

Carley assured him, "You won't be concerned about any of my players once you meet them. They're smart, sharp, focused, good students, dedicated athletes. I can't imagine any of them having anything to do with the coach's death."

"I'd like to talk with them. Could I come to your practice today?"

"Sure. It starts in about half an hour. Why don't you go to the Student Center next door and get a cup of coffee? I'll meet you back here in the gym and you can have as much time as you need."

Carley kicked off the practice session explaining to the women that Lt. Collins wanted to talk with them briefly, that it was perfunctory, and that they shouldn't worry about anything.

"Thanks, Coach Norgren. I'd like to take a few minutes to see if there is anything you can tell me that might be helpful. I just wanted to introduce myself to you. If you have any leads you think we should pursue, I want you to give me a call."

The women looked at him with blank expressions. Hanna was the first to speak. "You don't think any of us had anything to do with it, do you?" she questioned.

Smiling, he said, "I think that's unlikely, but it's my job to talk with anyone who might have any information. I can't rule anyone out yet. Here's what we think happened. You know how the scoreboard is mounted at the end of the court. It's a few feet below the ceiling, with two suspension cables holding it, and the electrical cables attached. But the scoreboard also has two maintenance cables, and it can be lowered close to the gym floor for repairs. Someone cut the suspension cables nearly through so that the scoreboard would swing down on the maintenance cables and hit the coach at the net. The apparatus the coach was standing on gave way. We don't know yet how the perpetrator released the scoreboard. But it shows premeditation. It was deliberate, and that makes it murder. If you know anyone who might be involved, it's important you tell us."

The women were quiet, seemingly overwhelmed by the conversation. Before he left, he asked Carley who would be knowledgeable about the workings of the gym. She brought him over to Vic's office, reassuring him she would be in touch if she learned anything.

Reaching out across the table to shake hands, Collins said to Vic, "I'm really glad to meet you. Everyone speaks very highly of you. They say you 'run a tight ship' and know just about everything that happens in this gym."

"That's true, I suppose. I love this place. Good kids come here. And athletes are the cream of the crop. I'm happy to work here."

"I'm investigating the death of the coach, as you probably know."

Vic nodded.

"And I have a few questions where I thought you might be helpful."

"Sure, I'll do anything I can."

"We think the scoreboard was cut down on purpose. Essentially, the scoreboard became the murder weapon. But it's an inconvenient one. Whoever cut it down probably thought no one would suspect it had been cut. How could anyone even get up that high in the gym?"

"Well, actually, there are two ways. We have the scoreboard inspected every year, lights replaced, all that maintenance stuff, and we usually lower it to the gym floor for that. There's an access point in the ceiling above the scoreboard for the suspension cables and the electrical wiring. It isn't very visible from here. Or, you could get a really tall ladder, and we have one. But that would be pretty tough and hard to stabilize. I'm betting on the ceiling access."

"I hadn't even noticed there was an access. Take me over and show me where it is."

Vic took him near the scoreboard. "See those ceiling panels? The one in the middle between the two cables holding the scoreboard is the false one."

"How does someone get up there?"

"There's a special entrance. I can show you. It's got a locked door, and behind the door there's a drop-down stairway." Vic pointed to the side of the gym nearest the entrance.

"Could you take me up there?"

"Sure, if you're not afraid of heights!"

"We're not going to be able to see all the way to the gym floor from up there, are we?"

Vic smiled. "Naw. I was just pulling your leg. The scoreboard is suspended on cables that are anchored to steel beams above the acoustic ceiling. We'll be walking along a platform welded to the ceiling beams. We won't be in any danger."

The two crossed the gym, with Vic directing Collins to a small stairway in the hall between the gym and the front entry. "It's right over there."

"I see the door at the top of the stairs has a lock. Is that door normally locked?"

"Yeah, we don't want any kids up there. Someone could have jimmied it. It's not much of a lock. Just enough to keep an inquisitive passer-by out."

"Who's got keys?" Detective Collins asked.

"I do, of course. So does the facilities department. They might have a couple sets, actually. Safety and Security has one in case of a fire or break in. And the athletic director has one. Maybe the coaches do, too. I don't know."

Collins studied the door intently. There was no sign of forced entry, but there were scratches on the lock. He couldn't tell if it was normal scratching from a key that had missed its mark, or something else. Vic opened the door, reached for a strap, pulled down a ladder, and began climbing up the steps. "When I get to the top, there'll be a ridge to stand on before we go all the way to the top. When you get to the ridge, pull up the ladder using this strap," he said, pointing to a leather strap on the top step. "That way, no one else can follow us up."

"It isn't a system for the faint of heart, is it?" Collins noted. He wasn't afraid of heights, but it wasn't the most secure structure he had been on.

When they finally reached the space above the gym ceiling, they maneuvered carefully across the metal floor, stepping gingerly over bolts and latches that secured the light fixtures. Light coming up through vents in the floor cast shadows throughout the upper deck. Through the vents, Collins could see the floor far below, shuddering at just how high they really were. Eventually, they reached the hinged access panel for the scoreboard. Collins could see there had been activity there recently Dust on the floor showed both footprints and handprints, which was both encouraging and curious. "Our investigative team said they couldn't find fingerprints when they were up here. This should have been secured as a possible crime scene."

Vic responded, "I've been up here doing some work, so those handprints are probably mine. I brought a couple of scoreboard vendors up here to take a look and give us an estimate for how much it will cost to replace it. You know, we didn't know it was considered a crime scene right away. I was just trying to get the dang scoreboard fixed."

Collins noticed that the support beam, midway between the suspension cables, showed a narrow band where dust was rubbed off. "What's that, do you think?" he asked Vic, pointing to it with his flashlight. "Could that be from a rope?"

Vic peered at it. "Yeah, maybe," he said. "Hard to say."

Collins laid his flashlight flat on the panel, trying to see if any rope fibers showed up. "Huh. If there are any rope fibers here, I can't tell." He picked up the light, and he gestured with it to Vic. "I've seen enough, I think."

When they were back on the ground level, Collins turned to Vic. "Wow. That was quite a tour. How often do you go up there?"

"Not very often. We change out all the lights once a year. They have to be broken in to burn at that intensity. We can do that from up there, rather than use a ladder from the bottom. Just lift up the fixture—they're hinged—and replace the bulbs. We do it over the summer when we can close the gym for two weeks and take care of the lighting before school starts up in the fall. We hire a student crew to do it. I'm getting too old to be climbing around up here much. I only come up when something goes wrong, which isn't very often."

"How long will it take to replace the scoreboard?"

"Oh, it'll be quite a project. All that information from the vendors is with Procurement now. We're hoping to get the scoreboard replaced before the basketball season starts, about a month off. I've been trying to light a fire under them to get it done. It's hard to operate with the old manual scoreboard we've got." He paused, looking up where the scoreboard had hung.

"Do you think this could have just fallen or is it pretty clear the cords were cut?" Collins asked.

"I was leaving that up to the manufacturer to figure out. They were here taking a look at it. They said it looked like someone might have tampered with the cords, but I figured they were just trying to cover their asses, pardon my French. My job is to get it fixed and make sure it doesn't happen again." He smiled.

"You know people connected with the coach. Who do you think might have killed him?"

Vic looked startled. "I have no idea. Volleyball is such a wholesome sport. It's hard to imagine anyone around here killing the coach."

"What about parents or boyfriends? Can you think of any that have hot tempers?"

"Well, sure. There's a lot of emotion for parents at this level of sports. I see it all the time. That doesn't mean someone would kill the coach. They might yell at him. But kill him? Naw. I don't see that happening."

"Who yells at the coach? Can you give me any names? I promise I won't assume they're murderers," Collins said.

"Well, the two loudest are Annie's father and Madison's father. But, like I said, they're good people. Just because they don't like what the coach did in a game doesn't mean they would kill him. Their daughters are great players and exceptional human beings. I don't think Madison's folks were in town the day he was killed."

"I have to ask. How about you? Were you in the gym the day the coach died?"

"Of course. We had a game that day. I left before the game to go and get a bite to eat. I wasn't here when it happened. I went to the submarine shop for a sandwich. Someone there should be able to back me up. They know me pretty well. I always get their meatball special."

"Thanks, Vic. If you think about anything I should know, anyone who's been hanging around the gym, anyone who asked you questions about the scoreboard, call me," he said as he handed Vic his business card.

"Will do," Vic responded. "Let me know if I can be of help."

16

The cell phone jarred Carley awake at 8 a.m. Feeling a little sheepish at sleeping in so late, she struggled to full alert.

"Is this Carley Norgren? My name is Bill Overland. I recently sent you an email expressing interest in producing a spectrometer using the patent that you hold. I was wondering if we might meet and talk about the potential and what I have in mind."

She responded. "I'm sorry I didn't respond to you right away. I was doing a little research on your company. Yes, I'm very interested in what you might propose. My brother, who lives in L.A., holds the patent jointly with me. I need to get him involved, and I haven't had a chance to talk with him yet. When and where do you want to meet? I have some schedule constraints right now. Is there any chance you could come here?"

"Of course. I can manage that. My operations are in Texas, but there isn't any need for you to see them just yet. We can make that part two of our exploration. I'll send you some dates, and you can see what you can work out with your brother. I'll wait for your call back."

"Thanks," she said. "It'll be soon."

Bill's company looked interesting. Unlike Manufacturtek, the company that had illegally produced a spectrometer earlier in the year using her father's patent, Bill's firm produced only spectrometers, mostly the type that took up a large room and required a dedicated air conditioning unit. The handheld spectrometer her father invented was small, relatively light, and could be used to analyze the chemical composition of liquids in all kinds of applications—agricultural, forensics, transportation. It was a pretty exciting breakthrough, but something she had no clue how to bring to market as a commercial product. When she was trying to get to the bottom of the patent fraud, she had hired an excellent patent attorney from Fargo and decided she would include her in the discussion.

Her brother wasn't in when she called. That didn't surprise her at all. Living in L.A., he had a very active lifestyle for a professor and was probably out enjoying an early morning run. He hadn't been back to the lake during the two years since their father's death, nor had she seen him in that time, even though they talked every other week. It would be good to see him in person.

When John returned her call later that afternoon, he was upbeat, "Hi, Lil' Sis. How are things going up in glorious lake country?"

She laughed, knowing that he actually didn't care much for lake country. He was more of an ocean person.

"I'm calling to see if you'd be willing to come up here for a quick trip. I got a call from a man named Bill Overland who is interested in offering us a royalty for Dad's patent for the handheld spectrometer. He'd like to meet with us."

"Well, that sounds better than letting the patent get dusty in a file folder. When did you have in mind? I'm teaching four courses this term, and it's a little tough for me to get away. But mid-term break is next Friday—maybe I could come up then. Maggie and I were going to try to have a long weekend get-away, driving up into the mountains. But maybe I could talk her into coming along. Would that be too soon?"

Carley was thrilled. She'd been hearing about the mysterious Maggie for months and couldn't wait to meet her. "It's not too soon in my book. I'll check with Bill."

"Or," John added, "you could come to L.A. Aren't you retired now??"

"You know I'm not. Plus, I have a new gig—I'm coaching volleyball at State."

"Well, la-di-da! Look at you! Let me guess how much you're getting—pennies per hour?!?"

"You should talk, Mr. English prof," she bantered back. "This could be our ticket to not having to be gainfully employed."

"I'm in. How will we figure out what the patent is worth?"

"I'm bringing in the patent attorney I hired to research the patent in the throes of things last summer. I like her—very sharp. Really helped us get to the bottom of things with Gordon."

"You are so smart, Lil' Sis. I'm proud of you. Yes, I'll be there. The Friday after next. How does that sound?"

"Deal. I'll text you when Bill confirms. You can stay in your old bedroom!" she said, chuckling. His old bedroom was the size of a large closet, with glow-in-the-dark star decals. "Just kidding. You can have Mom and Dad's old room. I'll look forward to meeting Maggie, too."

Bill quickly confirmed a time for that Friday, as did the attorney. What a huge help it would be to have something positive come of her dad's work. Her consulting contract was coming to an end, and she didn't want to get a full-time job while she was coaching. Maybe this could provide a little extra cushion in the meantime. The cabin wasn't winterized, and cold weather was coming soon. Maybe she could use the patent as collateral to take out a home improvement loan so she could get a new furnace installed.

17

It was Tuesday, the night the book club Carley had been invited to join was meeting at Betty Sue's home. As promised, Betty Sue had provided lettuce and chicken, while everyone else brought anything else they wanted to make an interesting salad—cheeses, berries, dried fruit, fancy vegetables, three homemade salad dressings—plus homemade bread and great desserts. It was elaborate and delicious. She already liked the group.

The women were all ages, bookended by Carley as the youngest and Betty Sue as the oldest. In between were women in their late thirties, forties, and fifties. Most of them worked, some of them were mothers, all of them were bright, energetic, fun.

Betty Sue interrupted the lively discussion going on. "I want to introduce the newest member of our group, Carley Norgren, who lives four cottages down from me. Her mother and I were great friends, and Carley has just moved back to the lake to live." Carley was relieved she hadn't included "jobless, loveless and homeless except for her lake home," true as that was. They went around the room, each woman saying something that would help Carley remember her. "Author," "Chief Technology Officer," "Mom of four and President of the PTO," "Nurse," "VP of Advertising," "Grandma and former CEO," "Entrepreneur," "Teacher," the list went on. Twelve women altogether.

Carley had actually read the book on team bus ride and during what little downtime she'd had during the day. As she listened to the women talk, she realized how hungry she had been for conversation with women. This summer she had been derailed by her tryst with Gordon and all that had happened in his wake. Now she spent her time with young women and Mark. Mark was wonderful. She had misjudged him when they first met; he had become a great friend to her. But no one could take the place of a close woman friend. Trish was her closest friend in the Cities. Trish who was getting married in January. Trish who was marrying someone Carley couldn't stand. Trish who was disappearing from her life. Carley missed her fiercely.

One of the women turned to Carley, "You know, you're kind of a celebrity around here. You helped uncover a major drug ring, took down an illegal manufacturing company, and identified a murderer. You've been busy!"

"I can tell you've read my press releases," Carly teased. "It was a big summer. I'm sure you saw what happened to my garage. My fall hasn't been much better."

They wanted to know more, and Carly filled them in on the coach's death, her team, how darling the women were, how terribly their season had gone.

"We'll come cheer your team on, if you let us know a day and time," one of them said brightly. "None of my kids were athletes, so it would be fun to adopt a team."

Everyone laughed and murmured in agreement.

"I would love that. I'll try to pick a good game," Carley responded.

It was a relief to be among so many wonderful women. She would be thrilled to call any of them friends. Locking glances with Betty Sue, she mouthed the words, "Thank you."

When the evening was over, Betty Sue asked, "Well, Hon, do you think you could have fun with us?"

Carley was surprised by the tears welled up in her eyes. "I've been pretty lonesome," she said. "Thank you for what you did for me tonight. I feel like I'm home."

18

Carley met Bill at the Fargo airport, his plane landing shortly before John and Maggie's. At 5'10", he was of average height and build, with a slight paunch, typical for men in their mid-fifties. His salt and pepper hair was beginning to recede. His eyes crinkled when he smiled, the lines on his face were soft, and he shook her hand with a grip that suggested a handshake was important to him. *Texan, but not a cowboy,* she thought.

"I'm really glad to meet you. My brother and his girlfriend are scheduled to land in half an hour. We can grab a cup of coffee while we're waiting," Carley said, pointing to the coffee shop near the entrance.

"I'm impressed," Bill said. "I fly in and out of Dallas all the time, and it's such a pain in the neck. This airport is much more manageable."

Carley agreed. It used to bug her when she was growing up that Hector Airfield only had two gates. Now it had expanded to five, and she hated to see it become that busy. Progress wasn't always progress.

As they left the coffee shop, she spotted John and Maggie walking through the checkpoint. Waving vigorously, she turned to Bill, "I'll be right back." She sprinted over to them, throwing her arms around John's neck and squeezing him hard. "I've missed you!" she said.

John hugged her back. "I've missed you, too. I'm sorry L.A. is so far away from the lake. Carley, I want you to meet Maggie."

Maggie was petite, about six inches shorter than Carley, with long, straight black hair and eyes with depth. Carley immediately hugged her. Maggie, looking a little surprised, smiled and hugged her back.

"Bill is over there. He just arrived as well. My car is right outside the building, and our meeting is at our attorney's office. We'll get your bags and go."

As they crossed the street to Carley's car, John and Maggie both marveled how fun it was to have the car parked that close to the terminal. Carley noted, "Small city life has its advantages."

"Accessible is a good word for Fargo," John said. "What a relief from L.A. We spent two hours in a traffic jam on our way to the airport this morning. I was afraid we might miss our flight."

"Fargo has a lot to offer. Plus, it's grown since we were kids. It's much trendier now—great restaurants, good art, and even an opera company with ties to the New York Met. I wasn't sure I would like it here after living in the Twin Cities for twelve years, but I really do."

Maggie took great interest in all Carley pointed out. As she listened to Carley, she commented, "I was born and raised in L.A. I could never imagine living anywhere else in the country. I probably would have made fun of Fargo if anyone had mentioned it as a place I might go. But this is pretty inviting."

"The people here are great, too," Carley added, as they got out of their vehicle.

Leslie Walker, the attorney Carley and John had hired to represent their interests, had offered the firm's conference room, about ten minutes away from the airport, for the meeting, and met them at the reception desk. After introductions were complete, Carley began the meeting. "Thanks, Bill, for coming all this way to accommodate my coaching needs. You, too, John and Maggie. Bill, why don't you tell us a bit about yourself and what you have in mind."

"I'm terribly sorry to learn what happened to your father. After his death, I researched his patents and discovered they had been transferred to someone else, or I would have contacted you sooner. When I learned all that had happened and that the patents were rightfully transferred back to you, I had to get in touch. Your father was a great man, and I'm sorry you've had to go through so much." Carley and John nodded silently in agreement.

Bill continued, "I met your father eight years ago at a conference, but our conversations didn't get serious until about four years ago. He had made some significant breakthroughs in spectrometry. I don't know how much you know about spectrometry, but it involves the diffusion of light through a substance to determine its chemical make-up. For instance, water treatment plants use a spectrometer to analyze what minerals and contaminants the water contains. No one had figured out how to make a device that was transportable. Your father did. It can be used to analyze a liquid in a bomb and determine what it is, for instance. A spectrometer used to take up a huge room and require its own air conditioning system. Now it doesn't. No one had figured out how to analyze black substances. He did that. In the past, black heroin was impenetrable for our technology. Now it isn't. He made such strides. We had talked about developing a joint venture, which was very interesting to me. While your father didn't have any business experience, he worked with people in several different fields to figure out what capabilities the spectrometer would need to have. He had a good sense of how to make things work. I thought the world of him. What we could have done together! It would have been sensational."

Bill continued, "Now, about turning the patent into a product. It will probably take about a year to fully commercialize the product—get it tested and get manufacturing in place. Your father has done most of the heavy lifting already. He had several prototypes which he had shown to a few key decision makers. They were gaga over it. That's what made it easy for Manufacturtek to step in. It didn't take much for them to get it up and running. Of course, we can't market it until we have a product to demonstrate. We expect sales to be relatively low the first year, probably around $500,000 or so. However, the demand for this product is very strong. We have significant interest from three major markets—Homeland Security, the Department of Agriculture, and the Department of Transportation. We project by Year 3 we'll net $10 million in revenue and by Year 5, around $30 million. And we think these estimates are conservative. I'm prepared to offer you an initial investment of $100,000 each, followed by a royalty on all sales of 5%. That would mean Year 1 would only generate royalties of about $25,000. But by Year 3 that becomes $500,000 for you two to share and $1.5 million by Year 5. We're good at what we do and are quite confident this product will be very, very successful. There are more applications than we have time to develop. However, as we develop technology that builds on your father's work, we would be willing to pay royalties of 2% to 4% on new products, depending on the investment required."

Carley and John looked at each other across the table. *Holy cow.* Carley was resisting the urge to jump up and down. John looked stunned. She was quite sure he had no idea what they had been sitting on. She hadn't, either.

"This is a very interesting proposal," Carley said. "Of course, we'd like to learn more about your operations and do a little research on our own."

Bill gave them a brochure about his company and talked to them about their sales strategies. Carley, who had always marketed technical products, was intrigued. "Could you give us a few minutes alone to discuss this?"

Bill replied, "Of course. I'll step outside and take a break. Let me know when you'd like me to come back in."

After he had left the room, their patent attorney, Leslie, looked at them both and said, "This is a strong offer. It's rare to get an upfront down payment before revenue has been generated. It's a sign of good faith and an encouragement to get you quickly on board. Five per cent is a reasonable, though not excessive, royalty for a highly technical product. You could ask for 6% if you wanted, but they might pull their upfront offer, and you would have to judge how that would serve you in the short run. If you don't need it, holding out for a higher per cent is, of course, the better option. Their offer of 2% to 4% on new products they develop using the technology is also generous, since you won't carry any of the risk for those. Actually, you might consider keeping the royalty at 5% and asking them to remove you from any product risk, since you have no background that could be useful here."

"I like him," John said. "I'd like to know a bit more about his company financials."

"He's agreed to share them with us once we've signed a confidentiality agreement," Carley said. "I think the next step would be for us to go to Texas to see his operation and meet some of his senior staff. Leslie, I'd like you to accompany us, if you would. That way, we aren't signing anything right now, and we have time to consider his offer and do more research on our own. We want to be smart about this. At the same time, I like him, I trust him, and I believe it's important to pursue this next step fairly quickly."

When Bill returned to the conference room, they agreed to a date two weeks out to fly to Dallas to see the company, meet senior staff, review more confidential information, and, hopefully, come to an agreement.

After dropping Bill off at the airport, Carley suggested John and Maggie tour Fargo while she held volleyball practice. They could have dinner at her favorite restaurant on First Avenue and make their way back to the lake after that.

When John and Maggie picked her up at the practice gym, John seemed amazed by Fargo's transformation into a sophisticated urban scene. "There are 25,000 college students in the Fargo-Moorhead area now. Many of them need English lit classes, John," Carley pointed out with a wistful tone in her voice.

John laughed, "You have a sales pitch, too, it sounds like."

"Maybe. I know you love L.A. and the ocean, but it's pretty sweet up here, too," Carley said. It was so good being with him. She hadn't acknowledged to herself how much she had missed him. The lake just wasn't the same without any family there.

As they entered the lake home, Maggie let out a little squeal. "Ohhhh. It's so cozy," she said. "The pine paneling and the rock fireplace make it so warm and inviting. I can see your family sitting around the big oak table in the kitchen, playing family games and eating big, comfort-food dinners."

John and Carley nodded. "Yep, it was pretty idyllic," John said.

They laughed as they took a look at John's tiny bedroom with glow-in-the-dark stars and put the suitcases in their parents' room. The bed was adorned with a large quilt made by their grandmother. Pictures of John and Carley from birth through adolescence adorned the walls.

"You can tell who the favorite child was by the size of the bedrooms," Maggie teased.

"Mine was built after John was gone," Carley said. "You know there's quite an age difference between us. My dad could afford to redo this attic by then," she said, with a sweeping motion of her hand. The windows on both ends of the bedroom overlooking the lake and the woods behind their property were expansive. "Plus, he did most of the work on it himself."

They spent the weekend lollygagging on the dock, kayaking and paddle boarding, sometimes all three of them together. She had borrowed one of her neighbor's kayaks. It was too cold for swimming, even though it was unseasonably warm for early October. Mark stopped by to say hi and had hit it off with John and Maggie, regaling them with FBI stories, at their insistence. And, of course, they had cocktail cruises around the lake on the pontoon boat, complete with Smedley-Medleys—their favorite cocktail of gin, tonic, St. Germaine, and lime.

When she took them to the airport, Carley choked back tears. "You're the only family I've got. And I hardly get to see you. Just because you let me have this cabin in the estate settlement doesn't mean you aren't welcome here any time. You are, you know."

John wrapped his arms around Carley as they stood at check-in and hugged her closely, while Maggie looked on. "I know. I've dreaded coming back, but it wasn't as painful as I expected. We both have great memories here. And you and I haven't spent nearly enough time together since you became an adult. I'm sorry I couldn't be here for you last summer with all you went through. You know, it was a condition of my summer teaching position at Oxford not to leave except for a family emergency. If I'd realized all that was happening here sooner, I would have come," he said, a hint of remorse in his voice. He continued, "You know, L.A. is a fun place to visit, too, and Maggie and I would love to have a chance to reciprocate, to thank you for your great hospitality. Maybe for Thanksgiving?"

She nodded, struggling to hold back the tears. "Plus, I'll see you in Texas in two weeks," she said. "By the way, you haven't asked my opinion, but Maggie is perfect. You two fit together really well. I'd like to have someone on my side to team up against you!" she laughed.

"Hopefully, there will be a wedding in our future. But not by Thanksgiving. So plan on at least two trips to L.A.," John said, smiling.

She squeezed him again. It had been a great weekend, she mused. Maybe she'd get a sister out of this.

19

After meeting with Bill Overland and spending a great weekend with her brother and Maggie, Carley was feeling ebullient. Driving back to campus, she thought about what the compensation from her father's patents might mean. She wouldn't have to race to find a job. Assuming things went through with the patent, she could take her time, perhaps figure out how to continue doing contract work so she could plan some travel and keep on coaching. She would still need to work—she wanted to work—but it took some of the pressure off. Her relationships with the players were building. They were looking more comfortable on the court and stopped by to see her between practices a little more frequently. She could get her lake home winterized, hopefully before the first snowfall. The electric baseboard heat she currently had to rely on wouldn't suffice in twenty-degree-below-zero weather. *And it really does get that cold up here*, she thought to herself.

Today the game was against an extraordinarily strong team, as most of their Saturday games were. She knew her players were better than theirs, but they had been so off-kilter their record was far worse. It was time to turn a corner, and she hoped this would be that time.

The players were psyched, looking more comfortable on the court. Carley called out the starters' names: Hanna, Caitlin, Brooke, Juanita, Madison and one of the sophomores. She talked to the others standing by the bench. "I want you to all stay engaged in the game. You do that, and I'll get you in. No more standing idly on the sideline. Look alert, cheer for your teammates, and I'll make sure you get some time." With that she held out her hand for a team fist bump. They all yelled, "Team."

The starters had a hard time settling in. Juanita missed a few serves that came her way and started looking sideways at the coach. Carley called a timeout and pulled Juanita aside. "I'm not going to pull you just because you missed a couple of balls. Relax. Have some fun. I've watched your tapes. You're the best libero in this conference. You just have to remember that."

When Juanita went back in, she missed another return, but quickly shrugged it off. She easily returned the next serve, one of the hardest serves Carley had seen all season. She gave Juanita a thumbs-up sign. Hanna was finding her groove in setting. She and Brooke—Batman and Robin, as Carley sometimes thought of them—were hot. Hanna would pass Brooke the ball with such a sleight of hand the opponents didn't know whom she was setting. Brooke, with her high vertical jump, lobbed the ball squarely between two of the opponents. The crowd of parents and friends went wild. This was the team they had been hoping to see. Madison was having some success, though she was still a bit erratic. After they won the first set handily, 25-14, Carley pulled Madison aside. "I'm going to give Annie a chance, but it's not because you've done anything wrong. I'm committed to getting everyone in. You're still my go-to outside hitter. I'll put you back in soon. I just need to get everyone stronger." Madison nodded in agreement. Carley substituted a freshman for Juanita as well.

By the end of the second game, all of the players had been in and had their "sea legs" under them. Hanna, Brooke, and Juanita continued to rule the court, but everyone had had some success. They won all three sets against a strong opponent. Finally, they were beginning to act like a team. Everyone left the court that evening in good spirits.

When Carley got home, she saw she had a text message from Jeff wondering how the match had gone and if she wanted to go out for a drink. She sent him a message back saying no, but thanked him. She hoped that was discouraging enough that he would get the message.

20

When her cell phone rang Monday morning, Carley was dismayed to see who was calling. It was Mac, her former "almost fiancé." She had seen him a couple of months ago when he returned boxes belonging to her that he had found in his basement, and it hadn't ended well. She assumed he was still involved with Kristin, the reason they had split. She'd finally let go of him, stopped stalking him on Facebook, stopped wondering how he and Kristin were doing. Still, she had no desire to speak to him now.

"Hello?" she answered in a monotone voice.

"Hi Carley. It's me, Mac. Can you talk for a few minutes?"

"Can I, or will I? Those are two different questions."

"I know, I know. I haven't handled anything well. Not the break-up. Not seeing you two months ago. I miss you, and I really want to talk."

"Well, I'm listening," Carley replied, tapping her fingers on the table near her.

"Not on the phone. I'd like to see you in person. Could I come up and take you out for dinner?"

"Dinner might be too much. How about meeting for a cup of coffee? You can tell me what you want to say, and I'll decide if it's worth any more time."

"All right. But I really want to have a longer talk."

"You mean, the one we should have had before you slept with Kristin?"

After a long pause, Mac replied in a subdued voice, "Yes. I've been a jerk."

"Yes, you have. If that's what you want to tell me, consider it said."

"I want you back, Carley. Nothing is the same without you in my life."

"But you're still with her, right?"

"Technically, but…"

"There is no 'technically' in my book," Carley interjected. "Don't call me again unless she's gone. And I'm not making any promises even then. I won't do to her what she—and you—did to me." Carley hung up the phone.

Carley sat shaking, surprised by how much the call bothered her. She could feel her face warming, a sure sign she was angry. Did she want to get back together with Mac? No. Then why was she encouraging him to break it off with Kristin before they talked? Was she trying to get even? She hoped not. Mac had done her a favor by revealing his true self before they took the next step into marriage. No, she shouldn't encourage him at all. Her trust was broken. Irretrievably, in her mind. How could she continue without trust? They had been together four years. That should have been long enough to figure out where and how they fit in each other's lives. She picked up her phone and texted him, *Ignore what I said. Don't break up with Kristin. There is nothing left between us. I'm not going back to you. Love the one you're with. And don't call me again.* After pushing send, she blocked his calls, texts, and emails, deleting his info from her contact list. She didn't want to hear from him again. Done.

21

At the office later that day, Carley pulled out one of the game DVD's she had watched a few days earlier. Something about the video bothered her. She played it until she came to the part she wanted. There was the young woman she hadn't met. This game was from the end of last year. The young woman was tall with long blonde hair, not unlike several others on the team. *Of course, over half of the population in this area is Scandinavian*, she thought to herself. *Maybe she graduated last year, but she looked young—eighteen-ish. Or else she decided to transfer schools. She was good.* It made Carley wonder why she left. A knock on her office door broke her train of thought. It was Hanna, the captain.

"Hi, Kiddo! Come on in," Carley said to Hanna. "What's up?"

"I need to talk to you about the game two weeks from now on Saturday. My sister is getting married, and I'm her maid of honor. I can't be at the game if I participate. I tried to ask my sister to get married after the season is over, but she couldn't wait. Her husband is in the military and may be deployed in November. So, could I go to my sister's wedding? Please, please, please?"

Carley didn't hesitate. "Yes, I think we could work that out. In general, I don't like to excuse players unless a faculty member absolutely refuses to budge on an exam or something. But a sister's wedding only comes around once. You're lucky to have a sister! And it's nice that you're close enough she's asked you to be in her wedding."

"Thanks. That's a big relief. I wasn't sure how Coach would have reacted. I'm glad to be working with someone reasonable like you."

"Say, while you're here, I want to ask you about this video. It's from a game near the end of the season last year, before you went into sectionals. Who is this woman?" Carley turned on the video that showed the tall, unknown blonde slamming the ball at the opponents.

"Mary. Mary Johnson."

"What year was she? Did she graduate from here?"

"No, she didn't graduate. She was a freshman—a first year we call them now. From Fergus Falls. She left after the first semester. I'm not sure why."

"Didn't she get along with the coach?" Carly asked.

"She did. At least he seemed quite enamored with her. He bumped one of the seniors for her position. But he often did that. Why?"

"Oh, I was just wondering. She looked like a strong player, and I was sorry we didn't have her on the team."

Hanna shrugged, saying, "Got it. Well, see you at practice."

Carley looked through the coach's files, trying to find information about Mary Johnson. She couldn't find anything. That wasn't a complete surprise, given that she had left the school. She wondered where she was now. Googling Mary Johnson and volleyball didn't produce a thing after she graduated from high school in Fergus. She was too good to not be playing any more. And Hanna hadn't said she was injured.

Later that day, Carley went over to the main administration building to talk with a secretary in Academic Affairs. "Is there anything you can tell me about Mary Johnson? She was a first-year student last year but seems to have left. I wondered if you had a telephone number for her or for her family. They're from Fergus Falls."

"That helps. We've had over twenty Mary Johnsons enroll here in the past three years alone. There are a lot of Scandinavians up here, as you know! I don't have a cell phone for Mary, but I do have her home number. Here it is. Parents are Linda and George."

"Thanks for your help. Is there any reason why I can't contact them? I'd like to find out where their daughter is playing volleyball now and what happened, why she left."

"It's all right, as long as you're on staff. Let me know if there is any information we need to add to her file."

"Will do." That was easier than Carley had expected. She could place a call to the parents to get Mary's cell phone number.

Back in the office, she dialed the number and was rewarded when a woman answered. Carley explained who she was and asked if she could get Mary's cell phone number because she'd like to talk with her about her experience at State. Suddenly, the phone went dead.

Startled, Carley sat back in her chair. Were they disconnected? Sometimes the reception in her office wasn't perfect. Or was she hung up on? Should she try again? In case it was a problem with her service, Carley redialed the number. The phone rang and rang, with no one picking it up. *Something must have gone very wrong,* Carley surmised. She hoped she hadn't made the situation worse. The woman sounded like she would be the age of Mary's mother. Perhaps, instead, Carley could find an email for Mary and see if she could connect with her that way. Or perhaps she should just leave it alone. What happened to Mary that would make her mother react the way she did?

22

The next day, after giving it more thought, Carley decided to see if she could track down Mary Johnson's email address. The only one the school had was the one she had as a student, using the school's domain. She would have lost access to that email after she left. Perhaps Admissions would have her high school email. *No one ever changes an email address if they don't have to, especially in college*, Carley thought to herself. About an hour later she succeeded.

Quickly, she dashed off an email to Mary, telling her she was the new coach at State, had watched her play, and wanted to talk with her about her experiences on the team. Would she be willing to call her sometime? She would love to chat. She clicked "SEND," hoping she could find out more sometime. Perhaps she could shed light on what was happening with the team. Maybe not, but it was worth a try.

Later that day, she checked her inbox. Nothing from Mary. *Oh well, it was a long shot*, Carley mused.

Practice that day was typical. No great breakthroughs. No awful experiences. Everyone still glum. They had an away game this weekend in Winona and had to make it an overnight because of the distance. She'd have to see if someone could take care of Abigail and Prattle. A quick text to Mark revealed he was willing. Good to have that covered. They would leave Friday after classes and return Saturday evening.

When she checked her email, she was pleased to see a response from Mary. However, quickly, her enthusiasm changed to dismay. Mary indicated she was living at home and unable to talk with her while she was there. Could Carley please send her a number where Mary could reach her, and she would be in touch? It sounded a bit "cloak and dagger" to her. Were Mary's parents mad at State? Had something gone down that no one knew about? It certainly wasn't flagged on her record. Carley responded immediately, giving Mary her cell phone number and times she would be available to talk. Now she just had to wait for her call.

23

A knock on the cottage door a few minutes after she got home surprised Carley and made her a little nervous. There was almost no one at the lake in early October, and she hoped it wasn't a man at the door. As she peered out a window, she was dismayed to see not only was it a man, that man was Mac. *Oh geesh,* she thought to herself. *Now what do I do?*

A thought of "*Just don't answer the door*" flitted through her head. But she was bigger than that. She opened the door, not saying a thing, her face deadpan, her mouth slightly downturned.

"I know, I know. You don't want to talk to me or see me. But please, I've driven three hours to see you. I really, really need to talk to you. Just for a few minutes even."

She stared at him through the screen door that separated them. "You didn't hear what I said when we talked? I thought I was pretty clear."

He responded in a rush. "I did. I did. But things have changed. Kristin saw your text and was furious when she realized I'd been in touch with you. She moved out. Said she should have known better. Anyway, that was four days ago, and I've spent a lot of time thinking. I really loved you. I still do. You were the best thing that ever happened to me. I miss you. I miss your sense of adventure. I miss your sense of balance. I miss how you make time for people. I understand why you don't want to see me again. But I have to try. I'm not willing to give up. I'll go to counseling. I'll figure out why

I wrecked the best thing in my life—you. I hurt you and I demolished us. Totally my fault, I know. Please. All I'm asking is that we talk. Not that we get back together. Can you give me some time to turn things around in my life? And maybe be open to where it might take us?"

Carley studied his contorted face. He seemed genuinely contrite, the first time she'd ever seen him that remorseful. He was in pain. While she felt empathy for his failure, she felt confused about what she wanted to do. Opening the door, she said, "One cup of coffee. That's it. Anything you have to say you can say while you're drinking it."

Breathing a sigh of relief, Mac came into the cabin. She put the coffee pot on the stove to percolate and motioned for him to sit down at the big, round oak table. "You look like shit," she said, standing by the stove, watching him, her arms crossed.

Her comment startled Mac, who shrugged his shoulders and said, "My life's a mess. I knew right after you moved out that it was a mistake. A mistake on my part, not on yours. Kristin is beautiful, and I let her beauty suck me in. But it's you I love."

Carley snorted, "Ugly old me?!? Aren't you generous." It wasn't a question.

Mac looked stricken. "That's not what I meant. It's just—well, you weren't around much for a long time. You left me on my own while you were dealing with people at work who had just lost their jobs. I knew it was traumatic for everyone when your company was bought out. But you abandoned me. And Kristin gave me a lot of attention. She picked up the slack from the difficult time you and I were having."

She felt her face heating up, her back to him as she poured coffee. "Are you saying it was my fault you were attracted to her?" she asked, handing him the cup, focusing hard so she wouldn't accidentally spill it in his lap. She faced him, still standing.

"No, that's not what I'm saying. I'm just trying to explain what was going on in my head. I didn't like it. I wanted to be the center of things with you. And I clearly wasn't. But maybe what I need to find out is why I always have to be the center of things for them to work."

That was more insight than she had heard from Mac in quite a while. "I appreciate your soul searching. I think that's a good thing for you. Especially doing it with a counselor who can help you get to the root of things. But there's been a lot of water over the dam, and my dam is pretty well broken. I'm not sure I can ever trust you again."

"I know, I know. All I'm asking is, would you try? Would you give me a chance to become the person I was when you fell in love with me?"

How can I say 'no' to that? She wondered to herself. *Can I abandon him when he is this vulnerable?*

She sat down across from him, the table between them, without saying anything for a few minutes. Mac looked down, humble, sheepish. Finally, she said, "Against my better judgment, I'm willing to talk to you again. I'm not promising anything. You get a counselor and meet with that person for several months before you call me back. I don't want to hear from you until you've had some new insights into what's going on with you."

"That's a long time. I don't even know how to find a good counselor. Can't we stay in touch in the meantime? I want you in my life, Carley."

She looked him in the eye. "You're a smart guy. You'll figure out how to find a counselor. And, after you start having some 'ahas,' call me, and we'll see how we're both feeling. That's all I've got for now. It's the best I can offer," she said, shrugging her shoulders.

"You're right. You're right. The ball is in my court to show you I mean it. I can do that." He picked up the cup of coffee, finished the last swig, and got to his feet. "I love you, Carley. I don't want to be without you. Thank you for letting me in."

"We'll see how this goes. Remember, no promises."

He went to kiss Carley, but she turned her cheek and leaned

away from him. She wasn't going to make this easy. She held the door open for him, resisting the impulse to bang it shut. She didn't look out as he drove away.

24

Minutes after Mac left, Carley grabbed two ice cold beers out of the refrigerator and headed over to Mark's. She should probably call first, even to find out if it was worth the trip. However, she decided to keep on going. She needed to clear her head.

Luckily, Mark answered the door and, seeing the expression on her face, said, "Uh-oh. Looks like someone's had a tough day."

"Oh, that's an understatement," said Carley. She held out a beer. "Do you have time?"

"Of course," Mark said gently, taking the bottle from her. "I'm not pursuing any bad guys today."

That made Carley laugh—the thought of him out rounding up bad guys was a funny image. She knew he did good work. It just sounded more cowboy-ish than he was in real life.

"What's up?" Mark asked as he led her into his small living room overlooking the lake. He offered her the one comfortable chair in the room.

"Mac. He just drove up from the Cities to talk with me."

"I thought you'd told him to get lost."

"I did. He just didn't listen. After the last time we talked, I texted him and told him to stay with Kristin. She saw the text I'd sent him and moved out. That was probably going to happen anyway. But he was so morose and contrite. He asked me to give him another chance. Said he'd go to counseling."

She paused as he said, "And how did you respond?"

"I told him to find a counselor, get through a few months and call me when he had some insights."

"You're tough!"

"I was badly burned. We had been very close. We did everything together, and I moved in with him about two years ago. It was after my Dad died. I suppose that had something to do with it. I was all alone." She took a deep breath. "I don't know—do you think people can change? On something like this? Someone who's cheated? Do you think they can resist cheating in the future?"

"If someone is really motivated, yeah, I believe it's possible to change. But they have to stay motivated because it isn't easy."

She leaned forward, meeting his eyes. "Have you ever cheated on someone?"

"How did this become about me?" Mark asked, laughing. "No. When I'm committed, I'm committed. It's not in my DNA to cheat. Not that I don't have other, equally abysmal faults," he said. "Loyalty is pretty important to me. That's probably why I'm in the FBI."

"How long has it been since you've been in a relationship?"

"Oh, so now we're getting really personal!"

She leaned back into the chair. "Sure. You know just about everything about me, having watched all my moves from the Gallagher cabin and from all I've told you about Mac."

"The last time I was in love was six years ago."

"That's a long hiatus."

"Yes, but it was a big love." He was quiet, with a small smile.

"What happened?" She prompted him gently, smiling back.

He paused, his smile fading. "She died. It wasn't anything big or dramatic. Not FBI related. It was cancer. She was in her mid-thirties, she developed breast cancer, and they couldn't stop it. She had a daughter whom I adore; she's a freshman in high school now. I see her every once in a while. She lives with her dad in Fargo. She's one of the things that keeps me up here. There. That was probably more than you were expecting." He raised his eyes to her, then looked away.

Carley exhaled a long breath. "Wow. I'm so sorry. I shouldn't have pushed you to tell me." She paused. "But I'm glad I did. I had no idea. That had to be excruciatingly hard."

He held the bottle up, studying it, not looking at her. "It was. Someone like her doesn't come along very often. We were in our early thirties when we met. I'd been preoccupied with my career before that and hadn't had time for a serious relationship. I dated a lot, but no one special. It was instant chemistry between us. We took it slowly because of her daughter, who was only six at the time. Now I wish we hadn't. We were married while she was hospitalized. She died two weeks later."

Carley let the enormity of what he had shared sink in. "Oh. Wow," she breathed. "That puts my love life to shame. I'm embarrassed I brought my sad tale of woe to you."

He smiled, looking a little rueful. "Oh, no! I can relate to sad tales of woe. But if I were you, I'd go for a man with staying power. Someone you can trust. Trust is a precious commodity. In my world, my life often depends on it. In your world, your emotional life depends on it. Don't get sucked back into something you don't want." He set the beer bottle on the table next to him and sat forward, elbows resting on his knees.

As she stood up, Mark got out of his chair. "It's getting late. I'd better go," she said. Trying to lighten things up a bit as she headed toward the door, she asked, "By the way, how do you like the new recliner we picked out?"

"I love it. Now I just need a couch and a dining room table. The legs on this card table are starting to give out," he laughed.

Carley noticed the weight of the papers he had piled up on the table was beginning to make one of the legs bow out slightly. "If that leg goes, you're in trouble. Maybe we should go looking soon?"

After setting a day and time for furniture shopping, she paused. "Thanks, again. Thank you for sharing the pain in your life.

I had no idea what you have been through. And thank you for the pep talk. I really needed that."

"Me, too. You were a good interruption."

As she reached over to give him a hug goodbye, he pulled her close to him tightly. Carley, patting his back gently, pulled back, smiled a quick smile, and headed out the door. He gave her a slight wave before he softly shut the door, watching her walk to the road.

Carley felt panic rising in her stomach. *What was that? Was that more than a hug? Did he just feel close because of the serious talk we had? Or is he interested in something more? And what if he is?* They had become close. But she knew she wasn't ready to face that possibility.

25

The next match, against one of State's archrivals, resulted in the first overnight the team had had since the first tournament in Illinois at the beginning of the season. It was a long bus ride to Winona, south of the Twin Cities—six hours each way. Each person was paired with a buddy to share a hotel room to save on expenses; it was the reason they all looked forward to the trip. They could count on late night talking and goofing around as a team. Since they had signed a pact not to drink during the season, it would be pretty tame.

The game didn't go well. The women were off-balance, even more than usual. The news that there had been foul play in their coach's death had the gymnasium abuzz with gossip. At the start of the game, one of the opponents laughed through the net, "How did you manage to bump off your coach? It was about time!"

Startled by the comment, Brooke took a step back and looked at Hanna. Hanna motioned to her to brush it off. It was hard for the young women to block out the commotion, and it showed in their play. It was their worst defeat yet.

After the game was over, the six starters retreated quietly to Hanna's room, sprawling out on the bed, the couch, and the floor. No one was talking. One of them turned on the TV for a distraction. Finally, Hanna turned it off. "We have to talk. We have a huge elephant in the room—that night in Illinois when we all were goofing around about how to knock off the coach. And now it's happened. The detective said the ref's stand gave way. And the scoreboard came out of the ceiling to hit the coach. It's exactly what we plotted. And now he's dead. But we didn't do what we talked about, did we?"

The young women looked guiltily at each other. Hanna reiterated, "We didn't do it, did we? Did anybody touch those bolts? You'd better own up to it now, before someone else discovers it. And you know they will."

Madison spoke up, "All right. I'll say it. I did it. I loosened the left bolt on the top step. I knew we didn't mean it when we were coming up with the plan. And I was sure no one else would do their part. I was just so pissed off at him that night. He was so rude. He knew my parents and my boyfriend were there, and he benched me. He humiliated me. I didn't kill him, though. It was only one step, for God's sake. That couldn't have done him in."

Brooke said, sheepishly, "I did, too. I was sure no one else would do it. It just made me feel vindicated. Like I could get revenge, even though I knew one step wouldn't hurt him. He might get a skinned shin out of it."

Juanita said, "Me, too." Everyone was nodding.

Hanna was dumbfounded. "All of us were in on it?!? Everyone did something??"

"Except you, it sounds like," Juanita said.

Hanna blushed, "Well, I did my part, too. We were all upset. He was acting like such a jerk. I did it to blow off steam. I tightened the net so if he fell onto it, it would hurt him. Never in a million years did I think he would actually be harmed. It just felt good. Like we could get even without anyone getting hurt. And now he's dead."

"Yes, but we tighten the net all the time," Brooke retorted. "You can't really think that would kill someone."

Hanna appreciated Brooke trying to get her off the hook. "I know, but that was my part. What about you, Caitlin? You were the one who suggested it. You're the one whose boyfriend works with the scoreboard. Did you have him disconnect it?"

"NO. No. No. No. I don't believe this," Caitlin sputtered. "We weren't really out to get the coach. It was a joke, remember? Sure, I told my boyfriend about the plan we'd hatched and how we'd get even. But I didn't ask him to do anything. I told him someone said how convenient it was that he worked with the scoreboard. But I didn't suggest anything to him. He wouldn't have done anything like that." Caitlin's voice was getting more and more agitated. "He's an engineering major, for Pete's sake." Realizing that was no defense at all, Caitlin abruptly stopped talking.

Juanita began to cry. "This can't be happening. Could we all go to jail for this? Could they figure out what we did? Did anyone see us? No one meant any real harm."

Hanna said, "Let's stay calm. I didn't see anyone do anything. Did anyone else here? That's pretty amazing when you think about it. At least six of us did our part, and we didn't see anyone else?" They all shook their heads.

"I don't know," Madison said. "I was probably the last one out of the locker room because my curly hair always takes longer to dry than anyone else's. I didn't see anyone."

Hanna responded, "That doesn't mean there wasn't someone else there who saw it. Like people from the stands. A parent waiting to talk to one of us. The janitor. Any of them could come forward to say they saw us tampering with the equipment."

Everyone sat frozen in place. The enormity of what they had done was hitting them.

Outside the door of Hanna's hotel room, Carley stood, back up against the wall, trying to absorb what she had overheard, not wanting to believe any of it, feeling slightly sick to her stomach.

26

The next day on the bus, as they drove home, Carley texted Mark. *What are you up to this weekend? Do you have any time to spare?*

I'm up to the usual—saving the world, defeating crime, dramatic home renovation, things like that. What's on your mind?

I need some confidential advice. Could you manage that?

Of course. Unless, of course, you're going to tell me something that has to do with a crime, then I'd have to act on it. But I'm thinking that's not likely what you want to talk about.

Thanks. I'd better find someone else.

Wait. You're saying it may have to do with a crime? It might implicate someone?

Yes. But I don't know yet if they SHOULD be implicated.

Let's not do this by text. I'll make myself available. Let me know when you want to get together. Are you okay?

Not really. I found out some things that no one knows I know.

This sounds familiar. Just like last summer. Let's talk. Call me as soon as you're back. Abigail Rose and Prattle send their love.

Carley sighed, shut off her phone, and put her head back against the seat. Her neck felt rigidly tight, and her temples were throbbing. She had a massive headache, and she hardly ever got headaches. The young women seated ahead of her were silent. Most had earbuds in, listening to music. Several were studying. They all looked like they'd been hit by a bus. Should she tell Mark? She couldn't believe that loosening a few bolts actually could have caused the coach's death. But were there any others in on it? Boy-friends, brothers or fathers of the players? Guys who could have controlled the scoreboard in a way to make it hit the coach? Is this something bigger? Did they think they were doing what the women wanted? Does that make it a conspiracy? Or did they consider it a prank? Should she confront the women? Maybe she shouldn't go directly to Mark. Could she be in any danger if any-one found out what she knew? There was a lot to consider.

Relieved to be back, everyone scattered when they got off the bus. As Carley headed to her car, Hanna intercepted her. "Coach Norgren?"

"Yes, Hanna."

"Could we talk?"

"Sure? If you want to talk right now, we can go back into my office. Is this a good time?"

"I don't know." She shifted uncomfortably from one foot to the other. "Maybe Monday. Could we talk then?"

"Of course. I'm available any time you need me. You can call me at home tomorrow if you want." Carley didn't know if she should pressure her. This was such unfamiliar territory. She didn't have a clue how to proceed.

Driving back to the lake in the fall afternoon light, the un-certainties bounced around inside her head. What would the re-percussions be of telling Mark? She didn't want to put him in a compromising position. She also wasn't sure she was ready to turn them in based on what she heard. Did she need to talk with them further? Did Hanna want to tell her? What was her responsibil-ity here? Someone should know. Someone who had the ability to pursue the truth further than she could. But if she believed they didn't mean to hurt the coach, was she required to turn them in?

As she pulled up, she was relieved to see Mark was nowhere in sight. She unloaded the car and greeted her two pets, who were only mildly happy to see her return. Mark had clearly given them plenty of attention while she was gone. She didn't want to talk with him just yet. Not until she had her head wrapped around what she wanted to tell him. It didn't matter. A knock on her door told her he had spotted her car in the driveway.

She opened the door. Mark was leaning against the door-frame, holding two beers in his hand.

"It's only three o'clock," Carley noted.

"That's true. But I can take what you say with a grain of salt if I think your judgment has been impaired."

"I don't know if I'm ready to talk. I just didn't know where else to turn."

"Knowledge is a heavy burden. Do you trust me?"

"You know I do," Carley said quietly, "with my life."

"Then why don't you trust me to do the right thing now? We can think it through together. I promise I will do everything I can to not betray that trust."

Carley heaved a big sigh. She knew he was right. She didn't know what to do with this information on her own. And she had a responsibility to help bring truth to light. She just wasn't clear about what truth meant here. "Can you be my friend first and an FBI agent second? I feel like that's asking an awful lot of you."

Mark looked at her for a minute and said, "If you tell me something I have to act on, I'll have to act on it. I can't deny that. But I will try to stop you from telling me something that might be too compromising. You need an ear. I'll be that ear for you."

"Come on in. We'll sit and look at the lake and talk."

She sat at one end of the couch and gestured to the other end. This might be easier if she didn't look at him. "Okay, here goes. We had a team meeting on Thursday after practice where I told the women what the police had told the school about the coach's death. It was clear they were all quite stunned. But no one said much. We had a meet in Winona, and the bus drive there was quiet. Our third game last night was especially awful. We lost 25-7, our worst loss yet. No one was playing well. Last night, I started a room check before I turned in. It's something I learned from my college coach. With a group of young women this age, you want to be sure they stay in all night. Ultimately, their safety is my number one priority. I started at Hanna's, the captain's room, and was just about to knock on her door when I heard some of the players in her room talking in frantic voices. It became clear to me that they had hatched a plan, some time ago. Am I about to say too much? Really, please stop me here," she pleaded, turning to him.

"I told you, trust me," Mark looked at her, his eyes locking hers.

She moved on the couch to face him, three feet away. "They were all mad at the coach after a game, and they wanted to get even. So they came up with a plan," she said, pausing. "A plan for how they might kill the coach. I can't believe any of them meant it. And I don't think they executed a plan to bump him off. They are all good people. They were mad at him for how he treated them. I've seen enough to know they had reason to be mad. Not mad enough to kill him, of course, but mad. They each had a screw or a bolt or a pin they were supposed to loosen on the ref's stand. And someone had pointed out that the boyfriend of one of the women knew what to do with the scoreboard. So, after their game before the coach died, each girl went and did her part, thinking they were the only ones doing it. Thinking that no real harm would come to the coach from loosening their one piece. It just made them feel better. The trouble is, many of them did it. This sounds like a conspiracy when I tell it to you. I don't believe the women were planning that something serious would happen to the coach. Whoever manipulated the scoreboard is the real culprit. I feel very protective of the players. It was a dumb, stupid idea. But it turned out to be the way the coach was killed." Carley looked at Mark expectantly.

He pursed his lips, almost whistling, and turned, looking out at the lake. Then he glanced at her. "Yep, that's a major bummer. And very complicated. The women may not have meant him any real harm. But it seems someone did. It's too big to be just a coincidence."

"I don't disagree. But if someone got the idea in his mind that he should do something with the scoreboard because of what the women had concocted, what are the implications for the women?"

"It's complicated. It depends on how involved they were or weren't. And it depends on the relationship to whomever released the scoreboard. And how much someone influenced that person or persons. Don't worry. I'm not prepared to turn them in based on what you've said, but I think there's more information to be had. You need to get Lt. Collins in the loop. If he finds out you have this piece of information and have withheld it, you can be charged with obstructing justice."

"I'm meeting Hanna on Monday. She asked to talk with me. I may know more after that."

"Don't tell her you overheard anything. Take it straight to Collins and let him decide what to do. Got it?" Mark asked, looking her in the eyes.

Carley nodded tentatively in response.

27

After Mark left, Carley checked her phone. She had texted Mary Johnson earlier to see if she would meet her for a cup of coffee, and Mary agreed to meet the next day, Sunday. Fergus Falls was only half an hour from Pelican Lake. She could easily meet Mary for coffee and still have time to get her yardwork done. She hoped Mary could shed some light on what had happened with the coach.

Getting to the coffee shop early, she settled into a booth and waited for Mary to show up. She wasn't disappointed. She recognized Mary as soon as she entered, as she had changed very little from her image in the game videos. Only now she was carrying a baby in a portable car seat. Carley had a hard time not letting her jaw drop. Why Mary had left State suddenly was very apparent.

"Hi! Are you Mary?" Carley asked.

The young woman nodded "yes."

"I'm Coach Norgren, the new volleyball coach at State. What a beautiful baby you have!" Carley said, trying to project energy, a smile, excitement. Mary seemed overwhelmed, almost indifferent.

"Thanks," she said as she sat down, maneuvering the car seat into the booth ahead of her. "I had hoped I could leave her behind, but my parents were going to a meeting at church, so I couldn't." She looked Carley in the eye and said, "Now you know why I left State and volleyball."

"She's beautiful. What's her name?" Carley asked.

"Leilanny."

"Ohhhh. Nice. It suits her. Is she named after someone?"

"My great grandmother."

"Is she your parents' first grandchild?"

"Yes, and they weren't happy about her as you can imagine."

"Let's get some coffee and you can tell me more. I'm buying," Carley announced.

After they settled in again with coffee, Carley said, "When I called to try to talk with you, your mother hung up on me. Is she upset with State? With the volleyball program?"

"She hated the coach and doesn't trust anyone connected with the volleyball program. When I started as a freshman, they were excited to see their daughter go off to the big university. I was the first one in my family to go to college. My older brother went to a trade school. But they were nervous, too. When I came home pregnant, they were very upset. I really let them down. They don't know who the father is. And that's the way I want it. They would have killed him."

"Is Leilanny's father still in the picture?"

"No."

"I'm so sorry. How are you doing with all this? It must be rewarding and challenging at the same time."

Mary's eyes welled up. "Life happens. I'm getting by." Her voice was low, sad, lethargic.

"I saw tapes of you playing volleyball for State. And I have to tell you, you were quite good. I wish you were still there. Do you play at all now?"

Mary shook her head. "No, I have way more important things to tend to."

Carley said, "I can understand that. It's been a difficult time at State, too. The coach's death has hit the team pretty hard, and the players are really struggling."

Mary asked, "How is Hanna doing? She's the captain this year, isn't she? She was my idol, always positive, such a good player. She watched out for all of us."

"Hanna's doing fine. The women respect her, and she's trying hard to pull them out of the doldrums."

Mary asked, "Are you enjoying coaching? I read an article in the college magazine that you're an alum. Pretty cool."

Carley nodded, watching her, coffee cup between her hands. "It is cool, but I also don't feel like I'm doing very well. The women have so much talent, but they're losing. I thought I might learn something from you about how I could help them. You are very talented and played a lead role on the team right from the start last year. Is there anything you can tell me that would help me do better? Anything about the players? About the coach?"

"He was an effective coach. I can't explain why. He was really hard on people, but at the end of the day you knew he cared about how the team did. The women were great overall. Some of them didn't like me because I bumped a senior. But I didn't do it, the coach did."

"Did you get along with him okay?"

"Yes."

Carley was struck by how abruptly Mary answered that question. "Did he ever pick on you or do anything inappropriate with you? Did he have anything to do with why you left?"

Mary jumped to her feet, grabbed the baby in her seat and said, "I don't know why I came. I was curious, I guess. I don't have any more to tell you. I didn't mean to waste your time. It's nice meeting you. I hope you have success with the women. I don't think I can be of any help to you."

Carley sat, dumbfounded, watching Mary quickly exit the coffee shop. She had really touched a nerve with Mary. Suddenly, there was only one question in her mind. *Is this the coach's baby?* She felt in her heart that her terrible question had been answered. Now what should she do? Why did Mary come to meet her? Was she looking for some resolution? And what might that resolution be? Carley left the coffee shop more puzzled than when she entered.

28

It was nearly time for practice Monday afternoon, and Carley hadn't heard from Hanna. She had sent her a text suggesting they meet at 2:30 before practice, but hadn't received a reply. She hoped Hanna would show up and that she would have a chance to ask her a few questions.

The clock on the wall ticked the seconds away mechanically. Carley was sure her heart was beating faster than the clock. Practice was scheduled to start at 3:00. At 2:55, Hanna jumped into the doorframe of Carley's office, out of breath. "Hi, Coach!"

Startled, Carley said, "Oh. Hi, Hanna. I've been expecting you. Didn't you want to have some time to talk?"

"Oh, it's all fine now. I just wanted you to know I figured it out on my own. No problem." Hanna breezed out of the door of Carley's office and headed off to practice.

Carley sat back, recovering from the whoosh that had just happened. Clearly, Hanna had decided against talking about her problem. What should her move be now? She wasn't prepared for that outcome.

Pulling together her lanyard with its whistle, her gym bag, and water bottle, Carley headed into practice. Although it was now 3:00, only a few women were in the gym. "Where is everyone?" Carley asked the players who were there.

Brooke responded, "A couple of people said they just couldn't make it today. Big exams tomorrow."

"What 'people' would those be?" Carley asked innocently.

Hanna looked around. "Well, Madison, Juanita, Annie and maybe two or three others."

Carley was afraid that might happen. "Hanna, get the 'missing people' on your phone. Tell them I expect them in the locker room NOW."

Hanna fumbled for her phone and started frantically texting.

"I said call them. We're not going to give them the chance to ignore a text."

Within five minutes, Hanna had reached each of the missing team members. She turned to Carley and said, "I'm sorry, Coach. They're not coming."

Carley thought for a moment, then stared Hanna down. "Let me tell you something. I came to your hotel room to do a bed-check Saturday night. I heard you together in your room talking about the incident with the coach. If they aren't here in 15 minutes, I'm calling the police. Now you get them on the phone, and you get them here." She surprised even herself with her toughness. She hadn't planned to reveal what she knew so quickly, but she didn't know what else to do and followed her instincts.

Startled, Hanna and Brooke called each of the missing players again. Within fifteen minutes, a very somber group of young women was sitting on the benches in the locker room, waiting for Carley to return. Most were wearing jeans, sweatshirts, and backpacks—not volleyball attire—and clearly had rushed to get there. When Carley stepped up to the circle, Madison jumped in, "You were spying on us?"

Carley took a deep breath. "Settle down, Madison. I'm not the one in trouble here." She looked at the haunted faces around her and knew what they had done had really taken a toll. "So I heard. I heard you were goofing around in a hotel room one night and came up with a plan."

Juanita tried to interject.

"Not yet, Juanita. Let me finish. I know you were mad at the coach. He was terrible to you. He yelled at you, pulled you from the game after one mistake, destroyed your confidence. I get all that. He was tough. And I think it made you feel better, blowing off steam, thinking of how you could get revenge."

Everyone nodded in agreement.

"But something went haywire. The coach is dead, and you are the ones who appeared to have plotted his death. Does that pretty well sum it up?" Carley asked.

"But we didn't really mean it," Juanita insisted. "At least I know I didn't. I had no idea that loosening one bolt would do anything, I had no idea anyone else would do her part."

"And it wasn't all of us. I didn't do anything," one of the freshmen countered.

Several young women murmured in agreement. The six starters looked very uncomfortable.

"But it happened, just the way you planned, and now we have to deal with that. No wonder you've had such a horrible season with the emotional baggage you've been carrying. Don't get me wrong. I don't condone what you did. But I also know you as the good young women you are. I don't believe anyone tried to kill the coach. However, *now* I need your help and your trust."

The women glanced back and forth among themselves. Finally, Hanna spoke, "What do you want us to do?"

"I think we have to let the experts sort things out here. You don't have to carry this burden alone. I have a close friend in the FBI."

Hanna Brooke, Madison, and Caitlin looked at her with disbelief. "You mean, Mark?"

"Yes. He doesn't think that loosening the bolts in the apparatus caused the coach's death. It might have aided it, but he doesn't think it would have caused it."

"You turned us in to the FBI?" Madison asked, wide-eyed.

"I didn't turn you in. Mark doesn't have any jurisdiction here. I just needed advice after I heard what you had plotted. You have been 'off' as long as I've been here. You are an incredibly talented group of athletes, but your performance says something has been getting in the way. I think we all know now what that something was."

The young women sat silently, staring at their shoes or picking at lint on the gym floor.

"I think it's time to be honest. You've heard the expression, 'the truth will set you free.' Well, that's pretty much how it works. I want to hear from each of you, then we'll decide what the best course of action is."

"We'll decide or you'll decide?" Madison challenged.

"I hope we can decide together. If not, it falls to me," Carley responded. "Here. I want each of you to take a sheet of this paper." She handed a pack of paper to Hanna, who was closest to her. "Write down everything you remember about what was said, who said it, what your part was supposed to be, and what you actually did. Then sign it. Start writing now. We'll take half an hour."

"Don't we get an attorney?" Madison asked.

"You aren't being charged with anything. This is just information gathering. Now start writing." Several reached into backpacks for pens.

Writing tentatively, the young women looked like cornered deer. But once they got past the first few words, the ink started to flow more freely. Meanwhile, Carley sent a text to Mark. *Oops. May have overstepped. 7 no-shows for practice. Made them come. Had them each write what they did.*

Mark responded, *Interesting. Not admissible in court. You went off plan, Nancy Drew.*

I know, I know, she texted back. *Just didn't want them all to run.*

Mark responded immediately. *Get everyone in the loop. NOW! Collins, president, athletic director.*

"*Will do,*" she responded, inserting a grimacing emoji.

She signed off, standing in front of the team, waiting to gather up their recollections, hoping she hadn't screwed anything up.

29

As she expected, the President and Athletic Director were stunned by what Carley had to tell them. *Stunned and disappointed I hadn't come to them first*, Carley thought. She explained that this was new territory for her. Before the meeting she had briefed Collins, who was quite surprised by the confession of the young women.

The first step, Collins thought, would be to bring Caitlin's boyfriend in for questioning. Of course, Carley expected that Caitlin would have already raised the alarm bells with him. Carley went through a step-by-step description of what she had learned and produced the sheets that the women had completed describing what took place after the Illinois tournament and what part each girl had played. "They are remarkably similar," Carley said. "I was hoping their stories wouldn't be wildly different."

"Of course, they might have agreed to their stories ahead of time," Collins pointed out. "And you know these papers aren't admissible in a court of law because of how they were obtained. You should have come to me first," he chastised her.

"I know that," Carley said, a little sheepishly. "But at least it gives you a sense of how they were just blowing off steam. Yes, they wanted to retaliate, but I can't imagine that anyone on the team really wanted to kill him or thought that would be the outcome of their small actions."

"We'll see," the detective said. His tone made her wonder whether she had done the right thing.

After the meeting had ended, Carley called Mark to see if he would be interested in a cup of coffee.

"I'm still in Fargo, and I have to wrap up a major report. Give me another 30 minutes, okay? I'll meet you at the coffee shop on Broadway."

When they were seated, Carley asked, "This is really big, isn't it?"

"Maybe yes, maybe no," Mark responded. "As I told you before, it depends on what is uncovered from here. On the surface, it looks like a prank. Each girl did her part to make herself feel a little vindicated, not knowing the others were doing theirs. Still, they may have contributed to manslaughter."

Carley blanched. "Oh God, I hope not. The futures of all these young women are at stake. They were just upset. I'm sure you can understand that. The coach was a jerk."

Mark said, "I'm well aware of that. But even jerks deserve to live. You know you have to be careful now, don't you?"

"Yes, but I'm sure that will be easier said than done."

Mark straightened a bit, his voice somewhat more professional. "If you see anything that the police should know, tell Collins. If you want to talk with anyone about it, talk it over with me. Don't go to the young women. I know you are quite an exceptional problem solver. But this problem has to be left to others now."

Carley nodded reluctantly. "I hope I did the right thing telling you in the first place," she said, hesitation in her voice.

"You did. In the end, assuming the man was murdered, things need to see the light of day. You have to trust that the truth will emerge."

Carley looked at Mark again. She was quite sure he was right. He'd given her a lot to think about. She was sure the truth would emerge between them, and she hoped she was brave enough to face that as well.

30

It had been an exhausting week with a lot of press for State. News about the coach's murder continued to make front page news. So far, word about the actions of the young women hadn't leaked out, greatly relieving Carley. The team members were subdued, but continued coming to practice. Carley told them that was important if they didn't want to appear guilty. They seemed more reticent around her. They must have felt somewhat betrayed by what she did. But she believed them. She had to hope things would prove her right.

Sitting in the coach's office, Carley wished she could find more information about Mary Johnson. She was locked out of the coach's email, but wondered if she might find something in his computer files. Opening his document files, she typed in the words, "Mary Johnson." Up popped a couple of recruiting letters from three years ago, but nothing more. She went under photos and did the same. Again, no files had Mary's name listed. There were all kinds of current team photos, but none of individual women. Scrolling through the list of files, she came across several from tournaments, including videos he had taken during practice and the game videos that were posted on the school's website. There were no recruiting videos, which seemed odd to her. She wondered where he kept those.

How she wished she could get into his email account. Checking to see if anyone was watching, she tried to guess what his password might be. "Coach," "state," volleyball." No luck. Cracking passwords apparently wasn't her forte.

Returning to the videos on the computer's hard drive, Carley picked out the one from the tournament the night before the coach was murdered. It was a very intense game, and the team wasn't playing well. The coach was in exceptionally critical form, yelling at the women at close range, benching them, storming out of the final game. Yikes, she would have hated to have been one of the players. It was abusive. How had the athletic director put up with that? Madison turned about four shades of red when he pulled her. The rest of the women looked despondent. She was sure it was pretty standard behavior for this coach. Wondering if he had always coached that way, she looked in the file directory and pulled up a video of a game three years earlier.

On the screen popped up a very explicit pornographic video of sex with a young woman. Quickly, she shut the file down, hoping no one had heard the sounds coming from the computer. Certainly it wasn't an acceptable practice to save pornography on a school computer. Now could she remember which file it was? She reopened the most likely one. She was right, and quickly shut it down again, making a note of the file name. What about the other videos? Is that what they contained?

An hour later she had opened every video she could find in his files. Six of them were pornographic. What a weird and risky thing to have done. One of the videos she opened actually was the video of the sectionals tournament from the previous year. The team had been defeated in the first round, even though they were predicted to be section champions. There was Mary Johnson, playing and attacking hard, no sign of pregnancy yet. She was the strongest member of the team. Carley watched the coach's interaction with her with great interest. Nothing, however, would make her think they were romantically involved. Perhaps she was wrong about him being the father of Mary's child. Was her imagination just running wild? Somehow, though, she didn't think so. She continued to study the game, watching the team get run over. Then she noticed something interesting in the background. The man she had seen at the Beach Volleyball game on Lake Sallie, the mystery man, the man the women said sometimes hung around the gym, was sitting in the first row of spectators. Something about him told her he didn't belong there.

31

Carley liked the athletic director, Brad, well enough, but wondered how he had put up with the coach's behavior. She couldn't believe his coaching techniques, especially yelling and profanity, were acceptable. There were sexual overtones, too, if not outright sexual harassment. Maybe she should wait until she had all the facts. On the other hand, it would be interesting to hear what Brad had to say. It might shed some light on how the team was functioning—or not functioning. And she had a favor to ask him. She called his assistant.

Brad's secretary confirmed he had free time that afternoon, and she jumped at the chance. When she arrived at his office, Brad immediately came out to greet her. "Hi there, Carley. I'm glad to see you. And twice in one week. It's my lucky week," he said lightly, ushering her into his office. "I really appreciate all you're doing and the care you're giving these women."

"I'm glad we have more time to talk, Brad," she said, sitting down. "It's been a pretty difficult few weeks. The women have struggled in volleyball, but now I understand why. It wasn't just the shock of losing their coach. They felt responsible for his death. But that's not why I'm here. You know I don't believe they are responsible. It was either a fluke that he died the way he did or someone else overheard them and bought into their fantasy. These are wonderful, thoughtful women. I am convinced they are innocent. What I came to talk with you about today is Pearson. What did you think about him as a coach?"

Brad looked at her carefully. "He wasn't an easy coach. But he usually got good results. Not so much with this team, but in the past he did well. He's got a winning record. Why do you ask?"

"Because I don't think much of him, based on what I've seen. He was a bully. He screamed at the women, sometimes using some pretty raw profanity. Didn't you notice it? Didn't parents ever complain?"

"Parents these days always complain. I take it with a grain of salt." He shrugged. "They can't stand it when a coach pulls their daughter or gets upset. Parents need to stay out of the coach's way. I always try to support my coaches. It's a different day today."

"Supporting coaches is a good thing, but screaming isn't, and it doesn't work. Not with women. Didn't you ever counsel him about it?"

"I can't say that I did. But we hardly had any attrition from his team. Wouldn't the players have quit if he were so terrible?"

"They are all athletes, and they wanted to play, but some of them did quit. What do you know about Mary Johnson?"

"Well, Mary Johnson was a special case. She was infatuated with the coach, at least that's what he told me. He assured me there was nothing going on between them. He never lied to me that I knew of, and I took him at his word. He was pretty religious, you know. I don't think he would have lied about that."

"So religious he wouldn't watch porn?"

"I doubt that he would. He went to Mass every day. He always said a prayer before games. He doesn't seem like the sort who would do that."

"Well, I found six videos of porn on his computer which I'm using now. It was pretty surprising. They're labeled as if they were games. But they aren't, trust me."

Brad sat up straight, eyes open wide for a moment. "Huh. Maybe someone gave those to him as a prank. He wouldn't do that on school property. He would know better. That'd deserve a reprimand, if not termination."

"Hmmm. Well, the files are there, on the hard drive I'm using. Stop by and check them out for yourself," Carley suggested. "And about Mary. I'd like to get her back into school and on the team. Would you help me with that? I'll need you to talk with financial aid. I've already talked to the childcare center; they can take her infant."

"Her infant? Mary had a baby? Well, I'll be darned. I don't know if you'll get very far with her parents. They were pretty mad at the school when they pulled her. I do remember that much. As I recall, they were mad at the coach and thought he had derailed their star daughter. But sure, I'll go to bat for her."

"Thanks," she said as she rose. It was clear she wasn't getting any additional information from Brad. The least he could do would be to help her bring Mary back. Was he blind to what the coach had been doing? Discouraged, she left for practice.

32

Within a couple of days, Brad had talked with financial aid and convinced them to reinstate Mary's scholarship. It wouldn't start until January. Carley knew it was too late for this semester. But she wanted to get Mary back no matter what it took, even if she didn't play volleyball. Mary didn't stand a chance in life as a single mother without a college education. She'd have to live at home for years. And, for some reason, home didn't strike Carley as a healthy place for her and her baby to be.

Calling Mary's cell phone, Carley was relieved when she answered. "Hi there. It's Coach Norgren. I'd like to get together with you again. Your scholarship has been reinstated, and I'd really like to get you back to school. The childcare center has an opening for an infant, and they said they would welcome Leilanny. I'd like to get you back on the team, too. Could we talk? I have some things to show you."

"Oh, I don't think my parents will let me go back. They've been great to Leilanny, and they think my life was ruined going to State."

"What if I talked with them? Do you think it would do any good?" Carley asked.

"I doubt it. But thanks for trying, Coach Norgren." Suddenly, the phone went dead. The conversation was over. Their family seemed to make a habit of hanging up on people. At least on her.

Carley was disappointed. She could use Mary on the team, but it was even more important to Mary and Leilanny's future that she get a college degree. She wanted to make up for whatever had happened between Mary and the coach. She hoped that wasn't too big a debt to repay.

Unwilling to give up easily, Carley drafted an email to Mary's parents that afternoon, telling them about the scholarship and the childcare center and asking for a chance to come and talk with them in person. She indicated she would call to follow up. When she did, two days after sending it, she got the familiar hang up. *Tough crowd,* Carley thought to herself. On the other hand, she didn't blame them. Their only daughter had gotten pregnant while she was at State. Her lingering question was whether they knew if something had happened between Mary and the coach. She wondered if they might have at least suspected foul play.

That night, returning to Pelican, she decided to drop in on Mark and see what light he might shed on the situation. After feeding her pets and taking Abigail out for a quick stroll, she grabbed two beers and headed over to Mark's. He greeted her at the door with a droll smile, "You don't have to bribe me with beer, you know."

"No, but then I don't have to hold anything you say against you," Carley said, reiterating the point he had made the day she told him about the team.

"Touché. Come on in, I just was finishing supper."

Carley eyed the remains of his frozen dinner and felt a little pang for him. "Another gourmet meal, I see."

"Hey, don't knock it until you've tried it. This brand isn't bad."

"You're spending a lot more time at the lake than I expected. I'm really glad you're here," Carley said.

"Well, things are pretty dull in Fargo right now. Being out here is much more interesting," Mark said, in his usual, understated way.

"I want to talk with you about a former player. Do you have time?"

"Always, for you," he said, a small glint in his eye.

Ignoring his slightly exaggerated tone, Carley described her experiences with Mary Johnson, the parents' reaction, Mary's quick exit when Carley pressed her about the coach, and her strategy to woo her back. "While I would like to have her on the team, I mostly want to make up for whatever may have gone down with the coach."

"Noble," Mark shrugged, "but not likely."

"If she were on the team and he had sex with her, are there any charges that could have been brought against him? Especially if it resulted in a pregnancy?"

"They aren't likely to be criminal charges," Mark said, "unless she was underage, which she probably wasn't as a college freshman. Or if it weren't consensual, which would be difficult to prove now. You'd have to talk with an attorney about civil charges. The school probably would have fired him if they'd known about it. And Mary might be awarded damages for predatory behavior by her coach. Actually, that still might be a possibility against his estate or against the institution. Has she admitted that he was the father?"

"No, but I have a very strong feeling that he is. I've watched his behavior on game videos with one or two of the other women. I know he plays favorites, and I've seen the look in his eye."

"That's not necessarily in the same league as fathering a child. Also, it would make a big difference if she felt she had to sleep with him to keep her scholarship or play her position."

"I don't know that she wants to share all that with me. Maybe she would if she returned and we developed a stronger relationship. Right now, she and her parents are leery of me."

"Maybe it's worth giving it another shot. Is there anyone they might pay attention to? The athletic director? The president?"

"I have no idea," Carley admitted. "I'll ask around." She looked again at the table, and then at the kitchen. "After you get furniture for this place, you should take a cooking class. It looks like you could benefit from some expanded horizons."

"Hey. I had a tough day. And what's not to love about a fully prepared turkey dinner?" He smiled at her.

"Someday I'll make you a real dinner. Then you'll know."

"Deal. Just tell me when."

On her walk back home, she thought about how much it meant to her to have Mark nearby. Of course, it wasn't just the proximity, though that was convenient. He had become her touchstone. His sense of what was right was a good compass for her. She could bounce things off of him without worrying about him betraying her or overreacting to what she said. *I think I've become important to him, too,* she thought to herself. She shook her head as she walked. *It's just too soon.*

The man with the binoculars watched her from behind his curtain as she passed by his house.

33

"Thanks for coming in, Hanna." Hanna shut the office door behind her.

"Sure, Coach."

"How are you doing? Are you feeling more settled?"

"I guess so. Everyone's just waiting for the other shoe to drop. We're all afraid that, any day now, we'll come to practice and all be taken away together in a paddy wagon."

"So far that hasn't happened. They're still trying to sort through who else might have been involved. I have a couple of quick questions for you. Remember that man you saw at the Beach Volleyball game on Lake Sallie? You said he sometimes hung out in the gym. Coach Pearson seemed to know him. Can you remember anything else about him?"

"No. He just always gave me the creeps. I don't know why. He never approached any of us or did anything wrong that we were aware of. Why? Did you see him around here?"

"No. I saw him in a game video I was reviewing." She paused. "What about Mary Johnson? What do you know about her? Do you know about her baby?"

Hanna paled. After a second, Carley asked. "So you do know she had a baby." It was more of a statement than a question.

This time Hanna nodded. "Yes, but I don't know much."

"Do you know who the father is?"

"No, I don't," she answered, looking very uncomfortable.

"Do you think Coach Pearson and Mary had a relationship?" Carley asked.

Hanna became very still. "I don't know. I heard rumors about it, but I didn't want to believe them. She is a very wholesome person. I didn't want to know if he was coming on to her. She took a senior's starting position, and there will always be someone making up stories to justify that. But Mary was a great player and deserved to bump her."

"Were any of the women close to her? She only asked me about you and told me how much she admired you."

"I can't think of anyone who was very close to her. She worked really hard at her studies. And at volleyball. I don't think that left much time for friends."

"Okay, but if you hear of anything or think of anything more, please tell me. And keep this conversation just between us."

Hanna agreed she would and went dashing out to the court to pepper the ball with Brooke.

I love these young women, Carley thought to herself. *They'd better be telling the truth...*

34

Ways Carley could support Mary began to take shape. She knew it was a long shot getting Mary back into school, but it was worth a try. She had other ideas she hoped she would be able to implement as well. But first, it was critical that she help Mary, whose life had taken a difficult turn while she was at State. Was she going too far? She hoped not. There weren't many opportunities for her to have an impact this big on someone's life.

Carley sent a text to Mary's cell. *I promise not to pry about what happened while you were here. I have some opportunities that I think could really make a difference in your life. They include a full-ride scholarship, care for Leilanny, and a place for both of you to live. Please, please, please let's meet so I can at least tell you more. You don't have to do anything if you don't want to. But at least hear me out. This could make a big difference in your future.* She hoped that might pique Mary's interest enough that they could talk.

It did. Several hours later Carley received a text back from her. *Okay. I'm not making any promises. Just tell me where you'd like to meet and when.*

A small sigh escaped from Carley's lips. *Let's meet at the same coffee shop. Are you available tomorrow—Saturday—around 10 a.m.? And please bring Leilanny. I'd love to see her again.*

Mary arrived, toting the heavy car seat with its precious cargo.

"It's good to see you, Mary," Carley said as she pulled up a chair. "And baby—they just don't come much cuter than Leilanny!"

Mary smiled, one of the few smiles Carley had seen from her. "She's just starting to smile. It makes it all worth it," Mary commented quietly.

After they settled in and Mary had picked up her coffee, Carley started in. "Let me tell you what I've learned. I asked the athletic director, Brad, to work with financial aid to reinstate your scholarship. He was successful. You could start second semester in late January if you're ready. You don't have to wait until next fall for the scholarship to kick in. Also, I contacted a nonprofit organization in Fargo that supports single mothers getting an education. They have three mothers graduating in December, so an apartment will available by January. Their facilities are beautiful—brand new, two-bedroom apartments. The support they have for their moms is unique. They have a childcare center in the building, counselors who are assigned to each family to make sure things are working out, shuttles to all three campuses in the area. You wouldn't even need a car. It's pretty astonishing, and they would be happy to meet with you or with you and your parents to tell you more.

"Why are you doing this?" Mary asked. "Is it because you want me to play volleyball? Is all this dependent on whether or not I play?"

"Of course, I'd like to have you play volleyball, but none of this is dependent on that. Your world unraveled a few months ago. I'm sure you had big plans for your college life and what you would do after college. I don't want to see you lose that. It isn't fair to Leilanny. It's likely she'll grow up in poverty unless you act now. You're a bright, talented young woman. And yes, I'd like to see State help you get back on track. Something happened while you were in school that derailed you. I'd like to be part of making things right."

Mary, suddenly teary eyed, looked stricken by what Carley had said. "No one has ever done such great things for me. I'm a little overwhelmed. I have to take responsibility for what happened to me. It's so much to process. I need some time to think."

"You don't have to answer me right away. You can take some time. Talk with your parents. Meet with the program in Fargo. Sort through what works best for you. Volleyball may or may not be part of that plan. See how things take shape. How does that sound?"

Mary nodded, sniffing quietly.

Carley said, "Now, can I hold that beautiful little girl? I promise I washed my hands before I sat down."

Mary nodded again, handing the bundle gingerly to Carley. "I need a restroom. Would you mind?"

As Mary walked away, Carley opened the bunting and looked fondly at the sleeping baby. Glancing up to make sure Mary had left the room and no one else was watching, Carley swiftly jumped into action. Removing the plastic bag from her jacket pocket, she quickly took a couple of fine baby hairs between her thumbnail and middle finger. As she pulled them out, Leilanny opened her eyes, but quickly shut them again. Carly put the hairs into the plastic bag and stuffed it back into her pocket. *Thank goodness Leilanny had some hair on her head. She might have been a baldy*, Carley smiled to herself. A few minutes later, Mary returned to see Carley gazing happily at her daughter.

"Thanks. I needed to think. What you've said sounds pretty wonderful. I didn't want to leave school. I just didn't know what else to do. My parents were so angry. They made me move home. I don't know how they'll feel about all this," Mary shared.

Carley said, "I'd be happy to meet with the three of you. This is a good school. You have a darling baby girl. What a great joy it would be to get life back on track for you. I know you're a strong student. It won't be easy, but I think you are tough enough to do it. Let's just keep the conversation going. We have more than a month before you have to make a decision about re-enrolling."

Mary nodded. Carley handed Leilanny back to her. "Thank you. It's been a long time since I've held a baby. You are very lucky."

Mary reddened a little. "I guess I am. I love her. There's just been a lot of turbulence over my pregnancy and her birth. I've felt pretty alone."

"What about the father?" Carley asked gently. "Do you talk with him now?"

Mary shook her head.

"You don't need to tell me more. Just know that if you make this step, I'll be there for you."

As they got up to leave, Mary gave Carley an unexpected hug. "Thank you for your belief in me."

Carley nodded. "Always."

35

"Okay, Okay, I'm pretty sure I did something that you're not going to like. And yes, it's very Nancy Drew-ish of me. But I think this could be key for what's happening with the coach investigation right now," Carley said, standing on the front step of Mark's doorway at his lake home, holding two beers.

"Geez, you know, we CAN talk without having alcohol involved!" Mark said, teasingly.

"A beer always helps a 'mea culpa' go more easily," Carley chuckled.

"Spill," Mark ordered. "Not the beer."

"Well, can I come in first?"

"Of course. What's going on?" Mark asked, as he directed Carley to the living room.

"I have a present for you. Actually, two presents." Carley handed Mark a beer, then what appeared to be an empty plastic bag.

"Okay, I give. What's this?" Mark asked, holding it up and peering at it, furrowing his brow slightly.

"You are going to hate this. I met with Mary Johnson, the girl I told you about who left State because she had a baby who is now about two months old. If you look closely, there are two blonde baby hairs in this little baggie," Carley said, wincing.

"Oh no, no, no, no, no. You didn't really do this, did you?" Mark asked, his voice insistent. "You know this isn't legal, don't you?" He took a long swallow from his bottle.

"Yes, I do. I did some research. I should have had Mary's consent. I know I was out of line. But it only matters if it's legal if something happens as a result of this test. We don't have to tell her what we learn. But if the baby is the coach's, you can request a legal test then. It gives you something to work off," Carley said.

"And what's your other present? I can't wait," Mark said, looking over his glasses at Carley.

She handed him another plastic bag with a hairbrush in it. "Yes, this is the coach's hairbrush. I found it in his desk drawer. Please, will you send this through your lab? If the DNA matches, we have a big twist to this story. If it doesn't, no one needs to be the wiser. What do you think?"

"I think you're pretty bold. Brazen, even. There is what's called a "chain of custody" we have to have for a DNA test to be legal. It has to do with all the permissions that are needed. And we have none of that. I know it could be very helpful to know if the result is a match with the coach's DNA. You went way out on a limb here, and I'm not wild about that."

She sighed. "I know. I have a very strong intuition about this. I didn't hurt the baby. She didn't even wince. I read up about it ahead of time, and I know you have to have a follicle from the hair to do the test." Carley explained.

Mark looked at her, shaking his head. "I don't want to get on your bad side. You're like a dog with a bone. You just don't give up. All right, I'll get it tested, but you have to promise me you won't say a word to anyone about this. Let me handle it. And, if there's a positive match, I'll find a way to encourage my friend, Lt. Collins, to run the test."

She laughed. "Thanks, Mark. I knew you wouldn't let me down," Carley said, giving him a quick hug as she left.

"Next time, ask me what I think before you drag me into something, all right?" He called after her.

"Promise."

Mark shook his head again as he closed the door behind her, looking as though he didn't really believe she meant it.

36

Carley was sitting in her office at the school the next Monday, completely absorbed in the tournament application she was completing online for her team when, suddenly, a large, imposing man with a booming voice stepped into the doorway, and bellowed, "Are you Coach Norgren?"

Instinctively, Carley rose to her feet, extended her hand, saying, "I am. And who are you?" she asked.

"I'm Mary Johnson's father. And I want you to leave Mary alone. She doesn't need this school. She doesn't need your help. She isn't going to play volleyball for you. Keep your nose out of our business or you'll be sorry," he said, almost growling.

"Please, Mr. Johnson, won't you have a seat? I'd really like to hear what you have to say."

"No. I'm not going to stay. I just came to by to tell you to BACK OFF. We don't want what you're offering. It's ludicrous to think Mary might play ball again. That ship has sailed. She needs to get a job so she can support herself and her daughter," he sputtered. His face was red and his demeanor menacing. She could feel anger radiating off him like the heat off the heat lamp in her cottage.

Carley held up both hands as if to stop him. "Please. Please. Just hear me out. The program she'd get into would provide childcare, housing, and support. And she doesn't have to play volleyball. That's not a condition."

"You're not hearing me. LEAVE HER ALONE. OR I'LL COME AFTER YOU," he shouted, wagging a finger in her face. Abruptly, Mary's father stormed away.

Carley sat down in her chair, hard, shaking all over. *What did he mean, "come after me"? Would he? Physically? Should I be worried?* It was such an overblown reaction, when she was only trying to help Mary get back on track. *Well, I'd better let it go for now. And what happened back at home? How was Mary faring with that wrath?*

Vic, the janitor, stuck his head into Carley's office. "You okay? I heard that man yelling at you. I wasn't going to let him hurt you. I followed him all the way out of the building and watched him drive away. I'm really sorry. You've been doing a great job with the team. I see you with them, and I can't help but think what a good change this has been. Hang in there. And if you see that guy here again, you let me know, okay? I'll defend you."

"Thanks, Vic, I appreciate that. He's just angry about what's happened to his daughter. I can't blame him."

"He doesn't know the half of it. You haven't done anything to hurt Mary."

"Oh, you know her? You know her dad?"

"Of course. I used to watch him in the stands during a game. I never miss any games, you know. He was pretty proud of her. But he didn't care much for the coach. A lot of us didn't. You're a breath of fresh air. You stick around, Missy."

Carley smiled at Vic. He was very loyal. Always was. He attended all of her games, too. And all of the basketball games and any other game that was played in the gym. He was its watch guard.

She decided she'd better let the athletic director know what had happened and picked up the phone. After he had heard her out, he said, "I tell you, Carley, parents are crazy these days. You tried. You did a good deed. I don't know what bee he has in his bonnet. I think he just wanted to get you to stop. I wouldn't worry about it. Who knows what's on his mind?"

His lack of concern surprised her. As she left the gym, she found herself looking over her shoulder. She wouldn't want to meet Mary's father in a dark parking lot.

37

Lt. Collins leaned back in the chair, studying Aaron intently. He had stopped by his apartment to ask him a few questions. "So, tell me why it is the volleyball team thought you might know about the scoreboard."

"I was part of the student crew that changed out lights last summer in the gym. And I run the scoreboard for some of the games, so I know it pretty well. That doesn't mean I am connected with what happened to the coach," Aaron said, an edge to his voice.

"You told me when we first talked that you were in the engineering lab when the coach was killed. I've checked. It appears you were there alone. I know you signed in, but you could just as easily have left and come back again. We don't have anyone who can verify your story."

"I could have left, but I didn't. Weren't you going to check cameras, too? There must be some way of verifying what I told you."

"Well, if there is, we haven't found it yet. So far, you're the one with the strongest incentive and experience with the equipment."

"I didn't have any incentive at all. The girls were joking around about bumping off the coach."

"You might have wanted to impress your girlfriend."

"I don't believe this. No, I wasn't trying to impress Caitlin. She's not like that, and neither am I."

"If I were you, I'd find someone who can verify you were where you said you were. Or find a good attorney."

Aaron gulped hard. If the police knew the whole truth, he could be in trouble. Maybe he could find a buddy who would stick up for him. He could see his future going down the drain.

38

Two days had passed since Carley's encounter with Mary's father. Mary hadn't called, and Carley didn't dare reach out to her. She hoped they would be able to talk sometime, but now was definitely not that time.

Caitlin appeared in her doorway. "Hi there. What's up?" Carley asked.

"I thought you said we could tell you what happened, and we wouldn't get in trouble," Caitlin said in an accusatory tone.

"Well, that's not exactly what I said. I told you if you *didn't* tell me what happened I would call the police. I'm glad all of you stepped up. It got things out in the open and made it apparent, I think, to the police that you didn't have any intention of really hurting anyone."

"No. You didn't turn us in, but you did turn in my boyfriend."

"What are you talking about?" Carley asked. She could sense Caitlin's increasing agitation.

"They brought him to the police station for questioning today."

"Did they bring charges against him, or did they just talk with him?"

"They've just talked to him. He has an alibi that I know will check out. I'm not worried about him. But why did you go to the police?"

"I didn't tell them I thought he did anything. They heard the story, and it's their job to follow up on any possibilities. You can't blame them for wanting to talk with him."

"No, but he blames me for getting him in trouble for something he didn't do," Caitlin sobbed.

"If he didn't do it, and I believe you when you say he didn't, he should be fine," Carley reassured her. She got up and came around the desk.

"Maybe he'll be fine, but he said he needs a break from me."

That stopped Carley. "Oh, I'm so sorry. This whole situation has been challenging. I'm glad the truth came out about the team. It was killing all of you to keep it inside. But everyone just needs to settle down and let the police do their job." Carley paused. "I'm sorry he's taking a break. From what little I know of Aaron, he seems like a pretty earnest guy. I'm sure he'll miss you. I don't think it's over for good between you. Just give him a little time. Once the police have verified his alibi, I'm betting this will all be a non-issue."

"He'd better come back. I came to this damn school because of him."

"I know. Hang in there, Caitlin. If I hear anything more, I promise, I'll tell you."

Caitlin left her office, cheeks stained with tears. *I had no idea coaching would be such an emotional rollercoaster,* Carley thought to herself.

The team was flat that day, and Carley decided maybe everyone needed a break. Their next tournament was Saturday, but she didn't expect them to win it anyway. They might as well recharge their batteries. Nothing else was making much of a difference.

When she got out to her car in the parking lot, she saw what had happened. A large rock now sat on the hood of her car, having bounced off the windshield, which was shattered. She was stunned. *This feels like more than a prank,* she thought to herself. Who would do that? Would Mary's father drop a rock on her car?

It was a frightening thought. Maybe he wanted to show her he meant it when he said he would come after her if she kept trying to get Mary back into school. Why would he have that reaction, when she was only trying to help? And, if it wasn't Mary's father, who would do that to her car? Aaron? Friends of Aaron? She called Security, who came and filled out an incident report. They told her she might be able to get a loaner car from the State fleet and gave her the name and phone number of the person to call. She'd have to get the windshield replaced and the hood fixed. What a bother that would be.

After a couple of hours, the fleet manager had her fixed up with a car she could use until hers was repaired. Grateful, she headed back to the lake.

On the drive home, Carley decided she'd better tell Collins about the damage to her car. He'd be able to check cameras in the parking lot and might find out who dropped the rock onto her windshield. Unfortunately, that wouldn't alleviate her fear of what was happening and who was trying to send her a message. She wondered if she should be worried that someone was coming after her.

At home, Carley found herself pacing. Abigail followed her nervously around the house, and Prattle moved back and forth agitatedly across her perch. *Why hadn't Mark or Collins told her they were bringing Aaron in for questioning? What if Aaron's alibi doesn't stand up? Then what? What if the DNA sample comes back with a match? Did Mary's dad suspect that?* She started to dial Collins' cell phone number.

Interrupting her cascade of thoughts was a knock on the door. She looked at her watch. It was almost 8:00 p.m. What if it was Mark? And what if it wasn't?

Peering out a side window, she was relieved to see Mark, holding a bottle of wine.

"I brought this to prove that not all of our encounters have to include beer," Mark said, eyes twinkling.

Carley wasn't feeling nearly as sparky as he was. "You sold me out?"

"What are you talking about?"

"Aaron, Caitlin's boyfriend. Collins questioned him today. Why didn't you tell me that was going to happen?" She took two wine glasses from the cabinet, and got out a corkscrew.

"Because I didn't know. Collins didn't share that information with me. He isn't required to, you know. I'm sorry he didn't. I would have given you a heads up."

Carley, prepared to do battle, felt the wind go out of her sails. "Oh. Well, I'm glad you would have told me. Did you hear what happened today with my car?" She opened the bottle as Mark stood watching her.

"No, I didn't. What happened?"

Carley said, "First, two days ago, Mary's father stopped by my office to yell at me. He told me to leave Mary alone, that she wasn't coming back, and I was ridiculous to think she could. He was screaming when he left. Even the janitor came to check on me."

"Oh no!" Mark said, with a look of concern. "That must have been frightening."

"It was. Then, today, I went out to the parking lot to drive home. My windshield was smashed in, and the rock that smashed it was sitting on my now-dented hood."

"How did you get home?" Mark asked, his brows furrowed.

"I've got a loaner from the school. I'll have to get the car towed in tomorrow. It's a little unnerving."

"I can imagine. Do you think it was Mary's father who did it?"

"I don't know. Could be him. Could be Aaron or some of his friends. I don't know how someone would know which car was mine unless they'd followed me. Someone wanted to send me a message, don't you think?"

"It would appear that way. Have you told Collins yet?"

"I was just going to do that when you knocked on the door," Carley said.

"Are you okay? Do you feel unsafe?" Mark asked, concern in his voice.

"Yeah, it makes me feel a tad vulnerable. I'm glad it was still daylight when I went out to the car. It's unnerving to be yelled at and have a rock dropped on your windshield."

Mark said, "No kidding. If you want an escort to your car, be sure to let Security know. If I'm in town, I'll come over, too. You have to be more careful now."

Carley said, "I'll keep that in mind. Thanks for your offer. I hope it doesn't come to that." She paused. "But you didn't come over here to check up on my car, since you didn't know what had happened. What brought you over here?"

A small smile crept across his face. "I came here with some news. A little drum roll, please."

"No. You got the results?!?? Already??" Carley asked, barely able to restrain herself.

"I did. And let me say, you should always trust your intuition."

"Ohmygosh. Ohmygosh. The DNA matched. The coach IS the father of Mary's baby?"

"Yep." He filled both glasses and raised his glass to her. She clinked hers gently against his.

"Wow. I hardly know what to say. That's so gross and yet so important to know. How do you think that went down? Do you think Mary was in love with him or did he coerce her? My guess would be the latter," Carley said.

"From what I've heard of the coach, I agree."

"I wonder if Mary's father knows or suspects. That wouldn't explain why he took my windshield out, however, assuming he did it."

Mark put his glass down. "Are you nervous? Do you think he would hurt you?"

"I don't think he would hurt me, but he's a big man and that, all by itself, is pretty threatening. You'd better make sure no one knows I'm behind identifying the father of Leilanny. How do you plan to handle it from here?"

"I plan to plant a seed with Collins. But if I do, he'll go straight to Mary for information. Mary is likely to think you connected him with her, and you might be hearing from the father again. Do you feel like you need police protection?"

"I don't, but maybe that's short-sighted on my part. Do you think Mary's father had something to do with the coach's death?"

"I don't know. It seems like a long shot that he would go to all the trouble to drop the scoreboard on the coach. But maybe he thought it would be seen as an accident. And it almost was," Mark said.

"This is making my head spin. How about another glass of that wine?" Carley said with a half-smile.

39

Carley had looked forward to lunch that day. She had contacted the coaches for the women's basketball, women's soccer, and women's hockey teams, all of whom were women, to see what she might learn from them. It was interesting that, of all the women's sports at State, only the volleyball coach had been male. Especially odd since there were almost no male volleyball teams in the Midwest outside of Chicago, certainly not in Minnesota or North Dakota. She hoped to learn more about the athletic director, the deceased volleyball coach, and get any help they could give her to navigate what was going on. They agreed to meet her off-campus for more privacy. She didn't want students to overhear what they might have to say.

Lunch was at an upscale restaurant in Moorhead. One of the coaches had said she would spring for the tab. As Carley recalled, it was the hockey coach. She assumed that must be the sport with the biggest revenue stream.

When the women arrived, Carley wasn't disappointed. Strong, vivacious, energetic women, all three were in their forties and had many years of experience in coaching. From the level of laughter as they entered the restaurant, Carley knew they had good rapport with each other. One was especially enthusiastic. "Carley, it's great to see you again!" It was Jan, the soccer coach. Turning to the other two she said, "I knew Carley when she was a student athlete here.

She was one of the best. It's great to have you back and leading a team again!"

Carley said, "Jan? I didn't recognize your last name! You must have gotten married since I saw you twelve years ago!"

"Yes, and I've had three children since then, too. It's wonderful to have you on staff here."

Martha, the basketball coach, spoke up. "You've had quite a time, haven't you? This has been a baptism by fire for you. I'm sorry we didn't think to reach out to you first."

Ellen, the hockey coach, said, "We've all been here so long we've forgotten how tough it is to be the newbie. And you've had a lot to deal with."

Jan nodded in agreement. "How can we help you? What questions do you have?"

Carley jumped right in. "Tell me about the coach. What was his reputation? Who were his friends on campus? What do you know about him?"

Jan responded first. "Well, he and I both coached fall sports, so I probably saw him the most. I don't know. He was quirky. He had a great record up until about two years ago. Things have kind of fallen apart since then. I've overheard some of the young women from his team talking in the cafeteria. It sounded as though they didn't care much for him. He was a good recruiter, but not a great role model or player developer."

Martha added, "That pretty well sums it up. He didn't hang out much with the other coaches. His closest friend was the athletic director, Brad."

"Well, that explains a lot," Carley said. "I've been trying to figure out how Brad tolerated some of the behavior I've heard about from the coach. Yelling obscenities. Playing favorites. Coming on to some of the women. Brad seemed oblivious. But the women are pretty aware of it all. Pearson was abusive at times. I didn't get the sense he was always like that. But he has been since most of this team has been playing. What's your take on Brad?"

Ellen laughed. "Brad is the epitome of a good ol' boy. He leaves us alone. He doesn't like to be challenged by a strong woman, so he just avoids us. That's been fine with the three of us. As long as we get what we need for our programs, we could care less what Brad thinks or says."

Carley said, "I found porn labeled as game tapes on the coach's computer. Brad pooh-poohed it and said the coach would know better. I've seen a lot of instances where the coach was screaming at the girls, and I'm shocked no one called a halt to it, especially in this day and age. I've discovered the coach had a pet, a favorite every year, usually a freshman. I think there's more, but I'm not certain yet or at liberty to talk about it."

Martha said, "No wonder someone wanted to kill him."

Carley added, "He may have gotten one of his players pregnant."

That got their attention.

Ellen whistled. "That's very serious. None of us were close to him. None of us have witnessed what this team has had to go through. At least I know I haven't. But none of us will miss him."

Carley asked, "How did the coach's relationship with Brad influence things?"

Jan said, "Coach Pearson got away with things we couldn't. He could overspend his budget. He could be gone more. As long as he had a winning team, he was gold. Things had started to unravel a bit in the last couple of years. But he and Brad were buds."

"I heard you had some scary things happening—an angry father and a smashed windshield," Martha commented.

"Good news travels fast. Yes, obviously I have upset a couple of people. Makes me wonder who the coach upset," Carley responded. "I'd like to stay clear of that one!"

The rest of the lunch was energizing for Carley. Clearly, these were three seasoned coaches who knew a great deal about both the ins and outs of the athletic program and how to motivate athletes. She could learn a lot from them. Actually, she already had. As they left the restaurant, they turned and waved. Martha said, "Be safe,

Carley. Watch your back."

Jan interjected, "And call us."

40

Carley was excited she and her patent attorney, Leslie, were meeting her brother John and Maggie in Austin, Texas, that Thursday, to tour Bill Overland's manufacturing plant. They'd successfully navigated the discovery phase. Bill's financials were strong, his reputation impeccable, and his distribution channels effective. *If everything goes well on this trip, we'll be signing with him*, Carley thought to herself. It was exhilarating thinking about her father's work coming to fruition in a legal—and lucrative—way. She wouldn't have to work, though she knew she wanted to continue. But it gave her flexibility over the next couple of years to continue coaching and begin building her own marketing consulting practice. Although the payback was small in year one, Bill's down payment would make her goal possible. She hoped nothing would fall through now.

It didn't. The factory operation, the staff, even Bill himself far surpassed their expectations. Bill was a strong CEO and his business was flourishing. It was exciting to think about their father's spectrometer patents coming to life and the financial security it would give her and her brother. Leslie was equally impressed and strongly encouraged them to move forward. By the end of the day, they had a signing ceremony, complete with a champagne toast.

"Dad would be so proud," Carley whispered to John. Nodding, John quickly wiped his eyes. She knew they were thinking the same thing—if only their dad had had the chance to enjoy the benefits of his lifetime of work. What a future he had created for them.

The return flight was uneventful. It was hard to say goodbye to John at the airport, but he promised, along with Maggie, a return to Pelican Lake next summer. The trip was also a good break from the intensity of volleyball, the coach's murder, and the team's vulnerability. At least she could settle in where she was, not having to worry about what her next step would be. She could do contract work part-time and continue to coach. If only her father could be here now.

41

On Monday, following a mediocre tournament, Carley checked her phone and was surprised to see a text from Mary. *I know my dad came to see you, and I'm sorry. He means well. He's very protective of me. And very angry at the school. But I've given it a lot of thought, and know what you've offered is huge. I'm really interested, and I'd like to talk more. Would you help me through these next steps? I'll have to do it without my parents' support. I'm 18 and legally can make these decisions on my own. I'm ready. Thank you for your great kindness.*

Carley immediately texted back, *Of course I'll help you. I'll get some appointments set up. Could you make it work tomorrow? You'll want some time to think things over. Maybe even talk with your parents about what you are deciding. And can you bring beautiful Leilanny? I could use a baby fill right about now!*

Mary's response was instantaneous. *Yes, on all counts! See you tomorrow, 10:00 a.m.?*

Deal.

Quickly, Carley jumped into action. She set up appointments with Admissions and Financial Aid and made a call to the non-profit in Fargo. Soon, everything was in place.

The next day, Mary came to her office, carrying Leilanny, and smiling the biggest smile Carley had seen.

"I'm so excited," Mary said. "It feels like a fresh start. I know you're right. I need to do this for Leilanny, and I need to do this for myself. It won't be easy, but good things never are. This is the first time I have felt like a cloud has lifted for me since I learned I was pregnant."

Carley gave her a little squeeze and said, "Here's the order of our appointments today. We'll end in Fargo, but still have time to come back here and debrief. Hanna asked if she could stop by to say hi before practice. So, if the timing works out, would that be okay?

Mary beamed. "Of course. That would be fun. I doubt I'll be able to play volleyball next year. But with a semester to get my legs back under me, who knows? I'd love to do it if I could."

Carley responded, "We'll cross that bridge later. None of this is contingent on you playing volleyball. Let's just take it a step at a time."

By the end of the day, Carley and Mary were both energized. In Fargo, Mary had seen the apartment, met other young women and their children, toured the childcare facility, and met with the program counselors. Staff had explained that she could get some subsidy from the state for food and expenses, as well as a childcare voucher that would cover the childcare center for Leilanny because of reciprocity between North Dakota and Minnesota. The rest of her living expenses and support would be covered by their organization. The facilities were immaculate and new—only a year old. She would enroll in a special class immediately to get ready for the big changes ahead.

"I'll have a great place to live, an outstanding center for Leilanny, support from the other women in the program, and you on my side. I never, ever expected life to take this great turn!" Mary remarked. "I don't know how I'll ever thank you."

"You don't have to. I only want what's best for you and Leilanny. You deserve that."

Back on campus, they returned to Carley's office to look at the course schedule. Hanna was waiting outside the office door. When she saw Mary, she let out a squeal. Blushing a little, Mary gave her a big hug. After they'd chatted a few minutes, Carley asked Hanna if she would mind getting things started with the practice. Hanna agreed.

"You can do this," Carley said to Mary. "I'll be there for you. Let me know how things go with your folks."

Mary assured her she would.

When practice was over, Carley pulled out the copy of Mary's application form for the Fargo program. There was a section for her to fill out, and she wanted to take care of it right away. Studying the form, Carley was touched by the paragraph Mary had written about why this program was important to her future and the impact it was already having on her confidence. Glancing over it to make sure everything was completed, one piece of information caught Carley off-guard.

42

Answering his cottage door with a smile, Mark said to Carley, "You, know, we have to stop meeting like his."

"I hope not! I have some new information," Carley said. "And it's big. I'm really glad you're home."

Mark ushered her into the living room. "And you didn't bring beer OR wine," he teased.

"This couldn't wait. I spent the day today with Mary Johnson and Leilanny. Everything's in place for her to move into the facility for single mothers and return to State. She needed someone to write a letter of recommendation for her to get into the program and gave me a copy of the application so I would have her background information. And guess what I learned?"

"You like these guessing games, don't you?" Mark said dryly.

Ignoring his teasing, Carley said, "Mary's birthdate is December 28th. She's eighteen now. That means Mary would have been 17 last fall, when she became pregnant."

Mark whistled. "Oh, that is big," he responded. "Very, very big. She can bring charges against the coach and possibly get a settlement from his estate. Wow. The jerk. Mary might not want this to come out publicly, but it might give her more resources moving forward. Shame on him," Mark said, shaking his head. "Have you told Collins?"

"Not yet, but I will. Now you know why I didn't stop at my place first. I couldn't wait to tell you. He's more than a jerk. This is a felony. I wonder if I can get Mary to talk to me about it."

"If you could, that would be the best option."

"Did I ever tell you I found pornography on the coach's computer, the one I use now in his office? I was pretty surprised by that. It was disguised as a game video, but it was definitely pornography. It seems like he had a pretty strong sex drive that he couldn't keep under control. I wonder if he's done this to other young women over the years. I suspect the answer is 'yes.'"

Mark's eyebrows lifted. "That actually might open up a different side of the investigation. Was someone getting even with him for what he did to a daughter or a girlfriend or a sister?"

"We might never know. Oh, I talked with the autobody shop today. They said it will take about three weeks to get the new hood installed and painted. I'm lucky I could get a fleet car from the school. Of course, it has 'State' written all over it, so I'll have to be more careful how I drive," she said, laughing. "That in itself is sweet revenge for someone. I wonder if they'll figure out who threw the rock."

"A lot of questions," Mark said. "Welcome to my line of work."

Carley smiled, "At least I have a car. Well, I'd better take off. Prattle and Abigail won't be happy if I'm gone much longer."

The next day, Carley called Mary. "How did things go? Did you tell your parents yet?"

Mary responded, "I did. They were pretty upset at first, but the more they heard about it, the more they agreed this could be the opportunity of a lifetime for Leilanny and me. Of course, it will be hard for them to give up time with their granddaughter. But it will probably also be a relief. I'm getting pretty excited."

"Me, too. I'm glad to hear all this. I do have something to talk with you about and wondered if I might stop by Fergus Falls to see you. No Leilanny this time. Would you be available Thursday at 10 for coffee, same place?"

"I am, but what's it about? Is everything going okay?"

"Oh, yes. Everything is working out great. I'll give you a copy of my letter of recommendation and talk with you about some additional possibilities."

"Sounds great. See you then."

Carley wondered if Mary would be as happy to talk with her once she knew what the topic was. And what would she do if Mary denied that the coach was Leilanny's father? She hoped she wasn't pushing too hard or too fast.

43

The young woman who entered the coffee shop looked nothing like the Mary Carley had met several weeks ago. This young woman had a bounce in her step, a look of exuberance, a sense that things were right with the world. Carley hoped this conversation didn't change that outlook. Mary glanced around, spotting Carley at a small table near the back of the coffee shop.

Mary gave Carley a quick hug, removed her coat, and sat down. "What's up? I can't imagine you've uncovered any more possibilities. You've already saved my life."

Carley gulped slightly. Could she press on? She felt like she must. She'd start with the good news. "Here's the letter of recommendation I drafted for you. I want you to tell me if you think this works." Smiling, she handed Mary a copy of what she had written.

Mary sat back and read the page-long recommendation as tears began to trickle down her cheeks. When she was finished, sighing, she looked up at Carley in earnest and said, "Thank you. I owe you so much. This is beautiful. I feel, on one hand, like you hardly know me. Then you write this and you nailed it. I am very, very grateful." She handed the letter back to Carley.

"Good. I'll get this in the mail this afternoon. There's something else I want to talk with you about. It's important, and it won't be easy. I need to know. Do you trust me?"

"Of course, I do," Mary replied.

"Would you hear me out, be honest with me, and not jump up and leave? I really, really need you to stick with this."

"You're scaring me, Carley. What would make me do that?"

"Well, what I'm about to ask you is very sensitive. There are several reasons I'm asking. Please, just promise me you won't leave."

"I won't, I promise. But what could be that difficult?"

"I'm using the coach's computer in his office. I came across some things that disturb me. What they suggest is that the coach had inappropriate relationships with some of his players. I need to know if he came on to you."

Mary became very quiet, looking down at her lap.

Carley, leaning forward in her chair, said, "Mary, I'm asking you a question that takes a lot of courage to answer. Please, will you tell me?" She paused. "Is the coach Leilanny's father?"

Mary turned completely white, then said, "I think I'm going to be sick."

Carley grabbed Mary's hand, "I am not asking this to put any blame or shame on you. I think the coach has done some exceptionally wrong things, taken advantage of people, hurt people. I think you are one of them. If the answer is 'yes,' it's not a judgment of you. It's about him. It's about whom else might he have hurt. And what responsibility he has here."

"But he's dead. What does it matter?"

"It matters because he had an estate. I don't know how big, but there may be resources that could come to Leilanny. For one thing, the estate may be required to pay child support. If he left no other heirs, then Leilanny may be entitled to whatever there is. That could make things easier for you and for Leilanny. That could make up for some of the deep pain I'm sure you experienced when he betrayed you."

Mary looked down at her hands in her lap, tears streaming down her face. "I can't believe you're prying into this. Please. Just leave me alone." She started to get up, then realized she had promised she would stay. She looked pleadingly at Carley, "Please, just let this rest."

"Mary, I saw the details on your application. You were only 17 when you started playing volleyball at State. I did the math. Given Leilanny's age and how long a pregnancy is, I think you became pregnant in November of last year. No matter what, that puts the coach in the wrong. You weren't of age. He was a predator. He may have told you sweet things, and you may have thought you consented, but there are reasons why men aren't allowed to have sex with underage girls. And you're proof of that, I am certain. Please, just answer me. Is the coach Leilanny's father?"

Mary sat, her face expressionless, her hands quivering, tears continuing to stream down her face. "He gave me a lot of attention. When I arrived at summer camp before school started, he took a special interest in me, told me he would make sure I had a lot of playing time. It was very exciting. I love volleyball, and to be able to play as a freshman was my dream. Then it escalated. He would give me hugs. He'd mess up my hair after we won games. It was uncomfortable, but nothing that really crossed the line. By October, he told me he was in love with me, that he wanted us to be together after I was done with school, that he would make sure I had a stellar volleyball experience. I think I got caught up in all of that. I saw him as my savior. I would have done anything for him. He started giving me very small kisses. Never when anyone else could see him. At first, I pulled back. But honestly, I liked the attention. He was smart, energetic, insistent. He kept telling me how special I was. By the end of October, he told me how much he cared for me, that he would never do anything to hurt me, that I could trust him."

"What happened after that?" Carley asked gently.

"In November, I was in his office just before Thanksgiving break. All of the other young women had gone home already, and the gym was dark. He was the only coach there. He took me in his arms, pulled me to the ground, and made love to me. It hurt. I didn't want him to do it, but I didn't know how to stop him. Our season was over, we'd been through sectionals. Afterwards, I tried to tell him I didn't want that. And he snapped at me. He told me I had led him on, that he had done everything for me, and that I had hurt him deeply. Hadn't he bumped the senior for me? And, of course, he was right. I had a spectacular volleyball career as a freshman because of him. I didn't know where to turn. I felt so alone. By Christmas, I barely made it through finals. I was so sick. When I went to the doctor, I found out I was pregnant. It was such a shock. I mean, we only had sex that one time. It was quick. It didn't feel like 'making love' at all. It felt awful. When I told him I was pregnant, he accused me of being unfaithful to him after all he'd done. And he told me he didn't want to see me again. Not ever. He told me I could fend for myself next year and I was off the team. By the time school started up again mid-January, I was two months pregnant and had to tell my parents. Of course, they were devastated. This was not what they wanted for me. I didn't tell them who the father was. I don't know if they had suspicions. They hated the coach. They knew he had told me I was done, and they had watched me play all season. They knew I'd had an exceptional start because they never missed a game. I was so confused. I didn't know where to turn. Oh, Carley, I never meant to lead him on. Yes, I loved his attention and the chances I had to play. I didn't mean to take advantage of that. It was overwhelming."

Carley leaned over, grasped her hand, and looked her in the eye. "Oh Mary. You've got this all wrong. This wasn't your fault. *He* went after *you*. This is what a predator does. No coach should *ever* have sex with a student. *Ever*. And you were only 17. That's a very vulnerable age, and the coach used that against you. He made you feel responsible. You weren't. He made you feel like you led him on. You didn't. It was the other way around. He led *you* on. Then he took advantage of you and had sex with you against your will. You know what that's called, don't you?"

Mary looked up at her, miserably, "I knew it wasn't right, but I didn't know how to stop him. He wasn't listening to me. He was in such a state. I felt that I'd brought that on. That I hadn't told him I wasn't going to marry him when volleyball was over. I just enjoyed the privileges our special relationship gave me. I felt guilty. Like it was my fault, not his."

Carley sighed, "It wasn't your fault, Mary. He was at fault. He was the adult. He had all the power. He knew exactly what he was doing. And he knew it was wrong. Otherwise, he wouldn't have waited until everyone was gone. I don't blame you. Not at all. The coach/player relationship has a lot of boundaries. He didn't. We need to hold him accountable."

"But he's dead, and it's my word against his."

"First of all, I believe you. Secondly, there are tests that can be run and, if they prove he is the father, that's enough. A minor is never responsible in this situation. Not ever. Not even if you really had led him on, which you didn't. Did you want this kind of a relationship with him?"

Mary shook her head.

"I didn't think so. He forced it on you, but he did it in such a cunning way he made you feel like it was your fault. I'm sure there are others this happened to as well. But, in your case, it resulted in a pregnancy, which I'm sure scared the hell out of him. You have many rights here. I don't know if he had resources, but a big share of what was his belongs rightly to Leilanny."

"Oh, I couldn't let this become public."

"He raped you, Mary. He was wrong. You didn't do anything wrong except enjoy volleyball and appreciate the position you held which, having seen tapes of you play, you well deserved. And, if you pursue legal action, the identity of a minor, which you were, is protected."

"Oh, gosh, then my parents would find out."

"Yes, but there are people who can help them understand that he was a predator. I'm sure he has some assets. He should pay. And the beneficiaries should be you and Leilanny."

"I'll think about it."

"Think about confiding in your parents. I'm sure they are good people. I know they are angry, and I don't blame them one bit. But, in my heart, I believe it would be good for them to understand what you've been through. There are people on campus and in your new program that could be helpful as well."

"Like I said, I'll think about it," Mary said, wringing her hands over and over.

44

Carley contacted Detective Collins about meeting to discuss the information she had gleaned from Mary.

Carley said, "Would it be all right if Mark were part of our meeting?"

Collins hesitated, "That's highly unusual. We don't typically involve FBI in cases that are this local. It's not a good use of resources."

"I'd like him to participate as a friend, not as FBI. He's been a big support to me and may have ideas of how I can be more helpful. I confide in him a lot. Please?"

Collins nodded. "All right, we can do it informally. I don't want others from my precinct wondering what's going on here." He knew his department would look askance at having the FBI involved in what was clearly their case.

Later that afternoon the three of them met in Carley's office on campus. "What have you learned?" Collins asked.

"I wanted to tell you more about Mary Johnson, the player who left after her first semester at State last year. A few weeks ago, I found out she had a baby. Yesterday, I was able to get her to open up to me about her daughter's paternity," Carley said, pausing. "The baby's father is the coach, just as I suspected. And Mary was seventeen at the time."

Collins blinked in surprise. He let out a whistle and said, "That certainly adds a new dimension to this case. If her parents know, that could be a big cause for revenge."

Carley responded, "She didn't seem to think they did. However, I certainly had my suspicions about who the father was early on. They may have, too."

Collins continued, "Pearson may have stalked other women on the team. There may be an unhappy parent or boyfriend who wanted to get even. Could be someone from a past team. At least now we have proof he crossed a line."

Mark added, "Don't forget, Mary Johnson's father was pretty upset that Carley has been trying to get Mary's scholarship reinstated and get her support as a single mother to finish college. Seems like he's quite a hothead."

"By the way, have you found out who dropped the rock on my windshield?" Carley asked.

"I checked the cameras in the parking lot where your car was parked by the athletic center," Collins said. "We didn't see the incident that happened, but we saw a car drive up in the vicinity of yours. I've got someone trying to blow up the film and see if they can learn more. I think it's a long shot." He continued, "By the way, I brought Aaron in for questioning, and it's not looking good for him."

"What do you mean?" Carley asked.

Collins was reluctant to say more. "You have to know this is all highly confidential."

Mark said, "We're both on your side. The more you tell Carley, the more she can watch what's happening around her."

Collins said, "I know. It turns out Aaron wasn't in the engineering lab when the coach was murdered. I got tapes from several parts of campus, and he turned up on one of them taken near the gym."

"What did he say about that?" Carley asked.

"He said he met Caitlin for a bite to eat before the game. Did she ever mention that to you?"

"No, but I haven't talked specifics with her. They've parted ways now, so she's pretty upset with me. He or his friends might have been upset with me as well. Hence, the windshield? I don't know much more," Carley said.

"When I asked him why he hadn't told me that when I first interviewed him, he said he didn't think I would believe him. Of course, now I don't believe anything he says," Collins said. "Perhaps the two of them teamed up. She was, after all, the instigator of the pin pulling. And he's pretty familiar with that scoreboard."

Carley shuddered. "I don't see her as that conniving. It's disconcerting that Aaron lied, I give you that. Now what?"

"Now I'll be following up with his friends, checking out the student union where he said they had lunch, and scanning other surveillance videos to get confirmation of where he actually was. What I still want to know," Collins mused, "is how the perpetrator reached the cables of the scoreboard to cut them in the first place. Whose key was used? Or did someone pick the lock? And why go to all that effort? Wasn't there an easier way to get rid of the coach?"

45

It was Saturday, and their game wasn't until 1:00 that afternoon. Carley was enjoying a leisurely morning in bed when her phone loudly jangled. She'd have to change the setting, but it was effective in a noisy gym. Dismayed to see the number that popped up, Carley answered, her voice flat. "Hey."

"Hey. How are things going with your volleyball team?" It was Mac, trying to sound chipper, not totally succeeding.

"Better. Not great yet. There's been a lot coming to light lately that's pretty difficult. I'd say this season is probably shot."

"Oh, I'm sorry to hear that. What's been coming to light?"

"It doesn't matter and I can't talk about it. How are you doing?" Carley asked, changing the subject.

"Better. I'm in counseling, like you insisted. It's been good. I know you asked me to wait two months to call you, but—"

"I told you to wait several months," Carley interjected. "It's only been one."

"I know, I know. I just wanted to have some contact with you. I'm taking it seriously, Carley. I've been working through a lot of things, like my parents' divorce. Like why I was attracted to Kristin, and especially why I acted on it. I'll be a better man because of this. I want to be a good enough man to win you back. I've started going to church again, Carley. I'm trying to get things right in my life."

Carley was touched by what he said. She hadn't realized how wounded he was while they were dating, though perhaps that explained why he was so reticent to make a commitment to her. "I'm glad to hear that, Mac. It sounds like a good start."

A long silence followed.

"I really miss you, Carley. You were the best thing that ever happened to me. We were good together. My love for you was genuine. We could talk about anything. I've told you things I've never told anyone else. We both liked similar things—art, classical music, reading, sports, long walks. We had great friends. We fit. I miss that. I miss your sense of adventure. I miss you when I go out for a run alone. I miss you when I'm sitting in front of the fireplace."

"I thought we fit, too." *And you should have thought about all this before you hooked up with Kristin*, she thought to herself. "I don't know if I can get past my trust issues with you, Mac. Certainly not this fast. It will take time for both of us. If ever."

"My counselor suggested we might consider couples' counseling if you would even consider talking with me about what happened. Unfortunately, that would probably mean coming to the Twin Cities."

"That would be tough in the short run because of volleyball. I don't know that I want to participate in counseling with you. I wasn't the one with a problem in our relationship. And counseling would take a commitment I'm just not ready to make right now. You keep on with it, and we'll see how things go in a couple of months," she said, delaying any decision. "I have to go. Bye." She had loved him deeply, and it was hard for her to justify not giving him a second chance. But her trust in him was shattered. Was it possible for her trust to be regained? *Do I care enough now even to try?* she wondered.

46

Later that day, Mark called. "Any chance you're up for a quick bite to eat?"

"As a matter of fact, I'm starving," Carley replied. "Our game this afternoon wore me out. We lost, in case you're wondering."

"I was. I'm sorry." Quickly changing the subject, Mark said, "I have a little low-key reconnaissance I'd like to do. And it's Halloween. What a combination!"

"Let me guess. We're going to the hotel-that-isn't-really-a-hotel, right? Where we saw the mystery man at the beach volleyball game? We'll sit at the bar, have a drink, ask around, have a bite to eat, see if he comes in?"

"If you get any better at this, we're going to have to put you on payroll," Mark said.

"I didn't think this was FBI jurisdiction."

"It isn't. Just trying to help a friend. And I'm hungry. If we happen to stumble over something in the process, so be it," Mark said.

Once they arrived at the hotel, Mark looked as if he were looking for someone he was joining. Telling the hostess they'd like to sit at the bar, he steered Carley to two bar stools and said, "I'll be right back. I have to use the restroom."

Carley sat at the bar, idly looking over the menu. When the bartender came up to her, she said, "My friend will have a Coors, and I'll have a Smedley-Medley—a gin and tonic with St. Germaine."

The bartender said, "Good drink choice. That's become pretty popular around here."

He returned quickly, the two drinks in hand. As Carley sipped hers, she glanced around the bar. A lot of retirees were there; she figured she and Mark were the youngest by several years. It was quiet now that the lake residents were gone. What a switch from how this place rocked at night during the summer.

When Mark returned, he shook his head. "No sign of him. I didn't expect we would see him. But it would have made this a lot easier."

Mark turned to the bartender, "I have a question for you. Do you have a minute?"

"Sure," he responded.

"Good. I'm FBI. In this drink menu, I've placed my I.D. and a photo of a man we're trying to track down. Be careful when you open it so nothing falls out. Would you please look at the photo and tell me anything you might know about him? I saw him a few weeks ago at the beach volleyball tournament. I have no idea if he's a regular here. But if you have any idea who he is, it would be extremely helpful."

The bartender nodded and, gingerly opening the menu, glanced at Mark's I.D. and the photo. "Yeah, I've seen him here. He'll sit at the bar, over there. Sometimes he comes in here alone, sometimes he has one or two other guys with him. I recognized one of them from the paper. It's that coach who died in that fluke accident. Let me think about a name for this guy. Maybe the manager can help. I'll be right back."

A few minutes later the manager came over, drink menu in hand. "I hear you're looking for someone. I don't want a scene. If you're going to make an arrest or if there's going to be trouble, I want a heads up first. Deal?"

Mark agreed.

"I'm struggling to come up with a last name, but his first name is Derek. We keep an eye on him, too. We think he's a bit player in drugs. Frontline. People come up, sit down next to him, chat for a few minutes, and then leave. He's smooth. I've never seen anything change hands. Doesn't mean it doesn't. Just haven't seen it. I called the police once, but he left before they got here."

"Is he from around here?"

The bartender spoke up. "I overheard him talking about fishing on Big Cormorant one day. He may have a cabin over there."

Mark thanked him and looked at Carley as if to indicate they could go.

"Hell, no! I'm starving!" Carley said.

Mark laughed. "They do have about the best burgers on earth here."

As they sat waiting for their food, Mark said to Carley, "Didn't the coach have a place on Cormorant? Collins must have that info. I wonder if there's a lake directory we could explore, looking near the location of the coach's place. Maybe the coach and the mystery man started out as fishing buddies."

"Good idea. I know Pelican Lake has a directory. I'm betting Cormorant does, too. A drug connection could explain why the mystery man looks familiar to you."

"Yeah, but he wasn't in our database, which surprised me. Or, with the beard, it might have confused the facial recognition software. In this picture, he has a scruffy one. Maybe he was clean shaven in our system. Some beards give more camouflage than others. Hard to know."

"And drugs. Very interesting. Do you think the coach might have been into them?" Carley shook her head. "Eesh."

"Possibly. The women talked about how explosive he had become. 'Steroid rage' is a thing. Some steroids increase the sex drive, too. Sounds a lot like the coach to me."

"Maybe the coach wasn't always a predator, is that what you're saying?"

"Maybe, though that's hard to believe," Mark replied. "He was a narcissist. The sex abuse took it to another level. He may have been abused when he was growing up. You never know what's in a person's past. No matter what, nothing justified what he did."

"Let's stop by the grocery store in Cormorant. If he has a place, I'm sure he'd shop there. Everyone does. They might know if there's a directory, too," Carley suggested.

"Sounds like a plan," Mark responded.

After they finished, Mark thanked the bartender and the manager and gave them each his card. They agreed to call him if the man showed up again.

"Do you think the mystery man could have killed the coach? Steroids aren't the big ticket that other drugs are, are they?" Carley asked.

"Don't kid yourself," Mark replied. "There's a lot of money in performance enhancing drugs. They aren't as well organized as other drugs, but they still rake in a lot of money."

Inside the store, Mark pulled out his badge and the photo of the mystery man, which he showed to the young man behind the cash register.

"Yeah, I've seen him. Why? What's he done?"

Ignoring what the salesclerk was asking, Mark pressed on, "Do you have a name? Does he have a place around here?"

"Yeah, I think he has a place on Big Cormorant. His name is something like 'Erickson.'"

"Last name or first?"

"Last. I don't know what his first name is, but I heard someone yell out his last name once when he was here. He's kind of a jerk."

"Is he ever with anyone when he comes in or is he pretty much alone?"

"Sometimes there's another guy or two with him. I know one of them—it's that coach who made the headlines in Fargo. The one who died in the net."

"Do you know who the other guy is?" Mark asked.

"Naw. I've seen him here, but I don't know his name. The three of them seemed to know each other pretty well."

"Thanks. I appreciate your help. Do you know if there's a directory of lake homes for Cormorant?" Carley asked. "I know Pelican has one."

"Yeah, but you have to go through the Cormorant Lake Association. We don't have a copy. There's information about the association officers on that blackboard over there."

Carley spotted the list of officers with their phone numbers and snapped a picture of it with her phone.

In the car, on the way back to Pelican, Carley said, "Well, that was a productive outing. There's a lot to follow up on here."

"I'll get a meeting together with Pete Collins, and we can formulate a plan with him. He needs to have this information, too." Mark was quiet for a moment. "By the way, why do they call the lake 'Cormorant'?"

"It's named for a bird. There may have been a lot of them around here once," she said. "Like the pelicans on Pelican Lake, which few people ever get a chance to see." She glanced over at him. "You know what a cormorant is, right?"

"No. I don't think we had any of those in Chicago," he said with a small smirk. "Are they songbirds?"

"Not at all. They're big black birds that dive into the water to get fish. Then they sit on a rock or a tree with their wings spread out to dry. The cormorant is a 'protected predator.'"

"Ironic," Mark said dryly.

47

It was the first Monday in November, and Mark and Carley had requested another meeting with Collins. Mark filled him in on their dinner at the hotel-that-isn't-a-hotel, including how they learned the mystery man's first and last names. "Carley contacted the Cormorant Lake Association for a directory. As soon as it arrives, we can search for this guy. I couldn't find him online."

"Interesting. You know, you need to let us handle things like this," Collins said, a slight edge in his voice.

"I don't disagree," Mark said. "However, because he appears to be dealing drugs and crossing state lines, he falls under my jurisdiction as well. Whatever we find out could help both of us."

Collins nodded slightly, shrugging. "What about you? Any news from you, Carley?" Lt. Collins asked.

"Not much on my end. Things have been quiet with the team. Can you give us any updates?"

"Again, this is highly confidential. I'm still checking out Aaron. After going up on the ceiling of the gym with the janitor, I'm more and more convinced this was a young man's crime. Or a young woman's crime. A young female athlete might have had the capacity to cut the cables that held the scoreboard in place. Annie Benson's father is of interest. His daughter has clearly been cultivated by the coach. He might have been onto that. I called him, told him we were contacting all the parents of the players, and asked if he was aware of anything suspicious. He said he was on his way to the game when the incident happened. I asked him how he felt about the coach, and he was pretty silent, then said, 'Fine." He didn't sound fine at all. He agreed to meet with me, so, hopefully, I'll learn more. There's nothing to say he couldn't have done it. Mary Johnson's father is still in the running. I'm thinking if we keep some heat on the young women, someone close to them might step forward, not wanting blame to be misplaced. Of course, I still want to know more about our mystery man. Carley, when you get the directory, would you please drop it off at my office? I'll take a look."

"Sure, I'd be happy to do that," Carley replied.

"One last thing, Pete," Mark added. "Could you have a drug test run on the coach? Or was that already part of the autopsy?"

"It wasn't, and, yes, I can have that done. Interesting. So, you think our mystery man may be into drugs and was the supplier for our victim?"

"Could be. It would be helpful to know. If the coach was doing drugs, we'd need to know what kind they were. That would help us figure out how likely a suspect the mystery man is."

"Will do."

After Collins had left, Carley turned to Mark, "It sounds like he's focusing heavily on Aaron, but I know Aaron. He's a pretty serious kid. I have a hard time believing he would hurt a flea."

Mark glanced at her. "I know what you mean, but he has to follow the evidence. Hopefully, our mystery man will have some potential."

"I know, I know," Carley sighed. "I'm keeping my fingers crossed that Derek's our man."

"Me, too."

Later that afternoon, Carley had a call from the president of the Cormorant Lake Association with the good news he had a directory she could purchase. She asked if he knew either the coach or a Derek Erickson. He said he knew the Pearson cottage. The coach inherited it from his parents about ten years ago. Erickson wasn't a familiar name to him.

After she picked the directory up, she brought it home. Prattle and Abigail were happy to have her there in the middle of the day. That hadn't happened much lately. Knowing smoke can be lethal for a bird, Carley moved Prattle's cage to her parents' bedroom so she could light the wood in the fireplace. Abigail came over and snuggled in by Carley's feet. Looking at the directory, Carley carefully scanned its contents. It was organized by beach and alphabetically by name. Looking for the coach's name first, she found the beach where his lake home was. Then she examined other names on the same beach. It didn't take long before—bingo—she saw the name D. Ericksen. Using the correct spelling, she found the property tax record for Derek Ericksen, Big Cormorant Lake, along with his mailing address in Fargo. She was right about that.

Curiosity overpowered her judgment, and Carley loaded Abigail in the car for a drive around Big Cormorant. It was a short trip, only five miles. Her GPS led her to the coach's cabin. It was an older cottage in very good shape, redwood siding with a dark roof. Probably three bedrooms, she guessed. The large yard was a bit overgrown; it didn't look like the grass had been mowed since the coach's death. Of course, now it was early November. Because the property had so many trees, the overall effect was rustic, not out of control. She walked up to the front door, which had a posted notice listing an attorney at a law firm in Fargo. She snapped a picture of it on her phone, thinking she could pass that information on to Mary. There was no sign of life anywhere.

Getting back in her car with Abigail, she verified the address for Derek Ericksen, which turned out to be just four doors down from the coach's property. It was a bit more unkempt, though larger, with a speedboat, a fishing boat, and a jet ski on trailers on a back lot. An ATV was parked behind a shed. She didn't go up to the door because a fancy car was in the driveway. *He has all the toys,* she thought to herself.

As she drove away, three cottages past Derek Ericksen's she spotted something that made her slam on her brakes. In front of a garage hung a sign that read, "Brad and Mary Anderson." Underneath the sign were little panels with the names of their three children. She hadn't noticed Brad's name in the directory. Pulling it out, she saw he was listed there as B. Anderson. It hadn't caught her attention. Here the three of them were—Coach Pearson, Derek Erickson, and Athletic Director Brad Anderson—all within a stone's throw of each other. *Huh*, she thought. *How...convenient?* She snapped a picture of his sign as well.

Quickly, Carley texted Mark, *Can you run Derek Ericksen (note the spelling) through your records? I think we've found our mystery man. Also, I found someone else of interest. When can you stop by? Will you be at Pelican tonight?*

I'll let Pete know, Mark texted back. *He'll want to run it through his records. I have to be a bit sensitive here. But yes, I'll run it through our databases, too. And, yes, I can come to the lake tonight. I was going to stay in town to catch up on a few things. But now you've got my attention.*

Carley was relieved he would be over soon. It was hard for her to sit on news like this.

Meanwhile, the man three doors down set his binoculars back on the cabinet. As he watched her drive into her driveway, he thought how good it was to see her back home, earlier than usual. She'd been gone a lot lately, and he didn't like that. Not at all. It felt like she had left him in the lurch.

48

"So what's the latest surprise?" Mark asked Carley.

"I told you I found Derek Ericksen on the same beach as the coach. I found someone else there, too. It raises a lot of other questions. And sheds some light on who the two men were with Derek at the bar and at the Cormorant grocery store."

"Are you waiting for a drum roll?" Mark asked, his eyebrows raised.

"All right, all right," Carley said, laughing. Then her tone became serious. "It's the athletic director, Brad Anderson. Seven doors down from the coach. Three doors down from Derek Erickson."

"Oh. That's cozy," Mark said. "That could explain why he didn't pay attention to some of the flagrant things the coach was doing. Didn't you ask him about the pornography and about what happened with Mary? Wasn't he pretty dismissive of you?"

"Totally," Carley responded. "The women coaches I met with said Brad just always looked the other way with the men. But I wonder, if the coach was into some kind of drugs, and Derek Erickson was into drugs, what about Brad?"

"That would make some sense. It seems hard to believe that fishing would be their only connection, especially with bigger fish in the offing. You'd better let Pete Collins know about this when you drop off the directory."

Carley wished that Mark could participate in the Tuesday meeting with the president along with Collins. She recognized the sensitivities there. Nonetheless, she felt uncomfortable being the bearer of such difficult and serious news. When she had accepted this part-time coaching gig, it never occurred to her what she might face. Certainly not this. They sat at a conference table near the president's office.

"Thank you for meeting with us, President Jenkins and Athletic Director Anderson," Collins began. "We have some important information for you about what was happening with the coach that you need to know. It isn't good."

"Well, the only way through tough news is through it," President Jenkins said. "Let's get started."

Collins and Carley then detailed what they knew about the coach's sexual impropriety with Mary Johnson, a minor, her subsequent pregnancy and dismissal from the team, the coach's potential sexual impropriety with Annie, and his defeated attempts with Madison.

The president responded, "I had no idea. This is the first I've heard of this. Why has it taken so long for this to come to light?" He turned to Brad, the athletic director, who looked very pale.

Carley spoke up, "The coach told Mary she had led him on, had made promises she reneged on, used him to get more playing time. He was very manipulative. He started when Mary was a freshman, away from home for the first time. It appears he did that with other women, too. If someone like Madison balked, he immediately stepped back. But he stopped using her on the team and made her feel incompetent, even though she was a strong player. He was smooth."

The president put both hands flat on the table in front of him, as though to anchor himself. His voice was rougher than before, almost a growl. "I am very sorry to hear all of this. I will have to make an immediate apology to the young women and their parents. I'll get our attorney involved; I'm quite sure there will be some kind of legal action out of all this. I would never have condoned his behavior in a million years. His winning record wouldn't have protected him if he were still alive. I appreciate you bringing it to our attention. That S.O.B." The president shook his head in disgust. Looking directly at Carley, he said, "What do I need to do for these young women?"

"I'm sure at least a couple could benefit from counseling support. Beyond that, we have to decide how much we tell the entire team. I'm on unfamiliar ground here," Carley said.

"We'll have to assemble a team of professionals to advise us. We'll need a plan that includes the Board of Trustees, student affairs, counseling, communications, and legal staff. I'll start that moving today."

"I expect Mary or Mary's parents will file charges against the coach," Collins warned. "I'm quite sure this will become public soon, and you'll want to be prepared for the fallout."

"Of course. We don't want to block any appropriate action. The last thing we want is to stonewall this. It happened. We condemn it. And we'll do our best to make amends for it. We will need to mobilize on several fronts at the same time. Thank you, Detective Collins and Coach Norgren, for coming to tell us this very difficult news."

As they walked out into the hallway, Collins turned to Carley and said, "I'd hate to be in Brad Anderson's shoes right now. He has a lot of explaining to do. And this will likely get tough for you. You could get trapped between the institution and the women. Or Brad might attempt to make you the 'fall guy.' You might want to hire an attorney to represent you, so you don't get caught in a tough position."

Carley gulped. That hadn't occurred to her. Here she had been advising Mary to bring charges against the coach, which she believed was the right course of action. She would always take the side of her players over the school. But she could see how that could get her into hot water. "Thanks," she said quietly.

49

Carley was lost deep in thought when a large figure filled the doorframe of her office. Startled, she looked up to see Mary Johnson's father. She leapt to her feet, backing up a few steps as she did.

"Oh, please, please. I'm really, really sorry," her father said. He held up his hands, palms out, fingers spread. "I came to apologize. I was so hard on you before. I hope you understand how angry I was. I'm not angry anymore. I'm especially sorry after all the good you've done for Mary. Can we come in and talk?" he asked, motioning toward his wife, Mary's mother, at his side.

"Of course," Carley said, breathing a sigh of relief. "Sit down, please. Are things going okay with you and Mary?"

"Yes. We're thrilled with the new plans," Mary's mother gushed. "We just came from Fargo where we toured the center where Mary is going to live, thanks to you. Beautiful new apartments, great childcare center, good support services. It's just what she and Leilanny need to get their feet on the ground. And we're welcome to come see them whenever we want. After all, Fergus Falls is only forty-five minutes from Fargo."

"And we're equally glad she'll be going back to school. We were so proud of all she had accomplished. She is the first one in our family to ever go to college. A college degree would give her a future she wouldn't have had if she went to work now," her father said, getting teary-eyed. "And the coach…" He struggled to regain his composure.

"Mary told us what happened with the coach. We never liked him," Mary's mother said, her lips pressed tightly together. "We should have guessed what he was doing. If only Mary had told us sooner." She sighed. "But I know she was overwhelmed. Mary said you told her she should contact an attorney about going after his estate."

"I did suggest that. I'm not a lawyer, and I don't really know what she'll need to do. It seems to me she should press charges with the police. Because she was underage and has proof he had a sexual relationship before she turned 18, I would expect the odds should be pretty good that she can get a settlement. I don't know anything about the coach's means, but whatever he has should go to Leilanny. And his lake cabin might bring a fair amount, given prices on lake property these days."

"We have a lot to learn. It's going to take courage on Mary's part to go after all this. But you've made her feel strong, confident, able to do just about anything. I still don't know about volleyball," Mary's father said, hesitating.

"I'm not worried about volleyball. It may not work at all for her to play, and I'm fine with that. If it does work out, that would be a bonus for both of us. None of this is contingent on her playing," Carley explained.

"That's what Mary told us. She said you've done this out of the goodness of your heart. We are so very, very grateful," Mary's mother said.

"It's the least I can do," Carley said. "Mary is a wonderful young woman, and both she and Leilanny deserve a bright future."

"Well, they have that now," Mary's father smiled, looking relieved.

As Mary's parents rose to leave, her mother grabbed hold of Carley and hugged her. "Thank you," she said, with tears in her eyes.

Mary's father took Carley's hands and clasped them tightly. "We'll never forget your great generosity. I hope you can forgive my missteps."

Carley assured them, "We're good. Thank you for coming to talk with me. You made my day."

After they left, Carley sat down, a sense of wonder flooding over her. That had taken courage on everyone's part. She hoped they had the tenacity to see this through.

50

She looked at Collins, whom she couldn't call Pete, though she didn't know why, and Mark. "What you're saying is that you have 4 or 5 suspects, none of whom are rising to the top of the heap."

"Pretty much," Collins responded. "Plus at least six of your twelve young women."

"By the way, Mary Johnson's father and mother came by to apologize. They said they hadn't known anything about the coach until Mary told them two days ago. I really hope he isn't responsible for the coach's death."

"Just because he 'played nice' doesn't mean I am willing to eliminate him just yet. And the women aren't in the clear either. While I don't believe they meant anything by their plotting other than tension relief, it's just too much of a coincidence. Did Aaron take their idea seriously? Did he enlist others to help him? Did the women conspire with the guys? We know of two possibilities among the parents right now, Annie's father, Jim Benson, and Mary's father. Were there others? Were any other team members approached for sex by the coach? We don't know that yet. And might one of them have had an angry relative or boyfriend? Then we have our mystery man. Was he supplying the coach with drugs? Was he romantically involved with the coach? So many questions. And, really, no answers." He paused. "But here's how you each can help. Mark, if you can continue to trace the mystery man through your drug contacts, that would be helpful. Carley, if you could find out from the women if the coach came on to anyone else, that would be helpful. I'm still reviewing videos on campus to see if anything proves or disproves Aaron's story. If you have any other ideas, please know I'm open!"

Carley said, "I'll ask around. The women may not be forthcoming. But I'll do my best."

Mark said, "I did get the report on the facial recognition software. The mystery man doesn't appear to be in our database. That doesn't mean he isn't connected with drugs; it just means he hasn't been arrested. Or else the software couldn't identify him. It's good, but it isn't perfect. Carley found porn with young women on the coach's computer. So I'm thinking it's not because the coach was into gay sex. I haven't seen anything that would suggest that."

"Oh, that's just a shot in the dark. A single man lurking around a college sports team where the coach is a man who wears spandex shorts? Sounds a little suspicious to me."

"Well, there are also very attractive young women in spandex. That might be an angle as well," Mark commented dryly.

Collins shrugged.

51

It was almost time for practice, and Hanna stuck her head inside Carley's office. "Hi, Coach! How are things going? Brooke and I thought we'd come over a little early."

"Good for you. Say, any chance you could stay for five minutes after practice?"

"Sure," Hanna responded.

At practice, the team was still unfocused, but everyone at least showed up. That had been Carley's biggest concern. Collins was scheduled to arrive any minute, and Carley hoped the meeting would go well. To get practice started, she announced, "I'm glad to see everyone here. I have some news for you. The lead detective on the coach's case is coming in just a few minutes. He has questions he wants to ask you as a group and questions he wants to ask of each of you individually. Everyone is to stay here until he's completely finished. You need to be very, very truthful and complete in your answers. Now is not the time to hold anything back. While you may be concerned about implicating someone else, we have to assume they'll be cleared if they're innocent. The school's attorney will be present as well."

Annie jumped to her feet. "I thought you weren't going to turn us in."

Carley replied, "I didn't 'turn you in.' But I had to tell Detective Collins what I heard. I like him. He wants to listen to what you have to say. In the meantime, we'll practice serving today so it isn't disruptive. Everyone is to stay in the gym until this is done."

On the other side of the gym, they watched a man walk briskly over to where they were all seated on the gym floor. "You all remember Detective Collins," Carley said. The players nodded. "He'll be using my office for the interviews. He'll be joined by Steve Blanchard, State's attorney." Carley wished her new attorney could have been present as well. He was in the same firm as her patent attorney, but they hadn't been able to connect yet. She knew State's attorney would look out for State, not necessarily for her.

"Hi," Collins announced. "I'm glad to have the chance to talk with each of you. Your coach told me about overhearing your conversation, but I want to hear it from you. If you know of anyone Coach Pearson had a conflict with or anything you've overheard, that would be immensely helpful. I'd like to start with the team captain. Which one of you is that?"

Hanna hesitantly raised her hand. "Do we all need attorneys?" she asked quietly.

Collins looked at her solemnly. "You're not being charged with anything. We're just trying to identify what happened. If you're worried that something will be said that may incriminate you, then, yes, you may get an attorney. However, we're just trying to get facts here. If we bring you in for questioning, that's when you should have an attorney present."

Hanna nodded.

As the two departed from the gym, the rest of the women started talking with each other in low, subdued voices.

"Come on, up and at 'em," Carley encouraged them.

Meanwhile, back in Carley's office, Collins asked Hanna to tell him, in front of Steve Blanchard, what had happened at the tournament in Illinois.

"Well, we'd had a terrible tournament. No one played well. The coach was angry with all of us. It had been a frustrating year that way. He was always going off on us. He picked on everyone. Well, almost everyone. The whole team was upset. One of the players suggested we get even and get him fired, but we knew that wouldn't happen. His record was too strong. So someone else suggested we bump him off. 'Bump' in volleyball means to volley the ball back and forth. It was all in teasing. We were laughing as we talked about it," Hanna blushed, realizing how bad it sounded as she said it out loud. "We didn't mean anything by it."

"Who suggested you 'bump' him off?" Collins asked.

"I don't want to say," Hanna stammered. "It sounds premeditated, and it wasn't. I know her. She was just goofing around."

"I need to know who it was. It sounds like she didn't mean it in anything except jest, but I'd like to talk with her more. She won't be the next one I interview, and I'll make sure she doesn't know this came from you."

"It was Caitlin. Caitlin Steffens."

"Is she the one who has a boyfriend who works on the scoreboard?"

"'Had' a boyfriend. They split up because of all the fuss about the coach's death. He felt she implicated him when he had nothing to do with anything. Anyway, yes, that was her boyfriend. But remember, we were just blowing off steam. It was fun to think about getting even. I don't mean it was fun thinking about killing him," she quickly inserted. "I just mean we were in a hotel room, plotting something we weren't going to do, and it made us feel powerful, when the coach had made us all feel so small." She hoped the detective understood she meant that.

"I get that it's fun to come up with a plot that no one's going to make happen. But it did. As I understand it, you each did your part."

Hanna thought for a while. "We did, but it wasn't like that. We weren't doing it together. Everyone did their part not knowing the others had done theirs. I don't know why it made me feel better. Do you know what we were each doing?"

Collins looked at her tentatively. "I've heard, but I'd rather hear it from you."

"Each one of us had a pin or a bolt to remove or loosen in the net or the ref stand. For him to be hurt would have taken a miracle. The likelihood of him dying from what we did seems really low."

The detective stared at her, saying, "Except that the scoreboard came crashing down. It appears that the coach may have lost his balance and fallen onto the equipment, which is what prevented him from getting out of the way of the scoreboard as it fell."

"Oh, geez." Hanna struggled with the realization of what he was saying. No one really meant any harm. She certainly didn't. How could she convince him? "Didn't you ever do anything where it made you feel better, where no harm was done?"

"This isn't about me," Collins pointed out. "I hear what you're saying. It's just such a strange coincidence that this is how the coach was killed."

Hanna nodded, her eyes clouded, playing absentmindedly with a piece of lint on her uniform, disbelieving that this could be real.

"Was there anyone else you can think of who had a motive to kill him?"

Hanna swallowed hard at "anyone else." "We didn't have a motive to kill him. Being tough on us wasn't a reason. We had a motive to get even," she said.

"Let me clarify, is there anyone whom you think had a motive to kill him? Anyone on the team? A team parent? A boyfriend? Someone on staff? Did you see him have a run-in with anyone?" His voice was more insistent, harder.

"No. No one comes to mind," Hanna said. "Parents would get upset sometimes at how he was treating us, but no one ever yelled at him or threatened him that I heard."

"Whom was he especially hard on?"

"Hmmm. He was pretty tough on Madison. She used to be one of his favorites, but not anymore."

"Did you think she deserved it? Did something happen?" Collins asked.

"I don't think *any* of us deserved it," Hanna said. "And I'm not aware of anything that happened with her. I mean, we all missed the ball, didn't get a play we should have, didn't get to the ball in time. She wasn't any worse than the rest of us. He would take it out on her faster. She'd be benched the minute she did anything wrong. There were no second chances."

"You said he picked on almost everyone. Whom *didn't* he pick on?"

"I meant everyone. I don't know. Usually he didn't pick on Annie, but lately he even did that."

After a few more minutes, Collins thanked her and walked back out into the gym with her. "Thanks, Hanna. I'm going to continue with the seniors. Brooke, that means you're up next," he said, looking at the list and motioning her toward Carley's office.

After Brooke had described what had happened after the game, Collins asked, "When you did your part, did anyone see you? Was there anyone else in the gym?"

Brooke responded, "No. I was all alone."

Collins pressed on. "Isn't that kind of unusual? Don't you usually leave the gym as a group?"

"Not really. Some girls take longer to get ready than others. I don't wear any make up, so I'm usually one of the first out of the locker room."

"Did you tell anyone what you'd done?"

"I didn't. It wasn't that big a deal. It just felt like a sisterhood thing, you know? We're all in this together. Only no one else was in on it, really."

"Can you think of anyone else who might like to see your coach dead?"

"I don't know. Maybe some past players? He's got quite a reputation."

"Any names?"

"No. I'm just grasping at straws. I really don't know anyone who would kill the coach. At least, I hope I don't."

Collins leaned back in Carley's chair. "Ask Caitlin to come in now, would you?" Brooke stood, stepping almost woodenly to the door.

A knock came two minutes later. Caitlin peeked tentatively into the office. "You ready for me?" she asked.

"I am," Collins replied. "Come, sit down. Let's start by talking about what happened at the game."

Caitlin immediately burst into tears. "I know you think I was the mastermind behind all this. And I don't deny that it was my idea. But there was no plot. We were just goofing around. Now the coach is dead and my boyfriend has left me. I never tried to involve him in anything. Please, you've got to believe me!"

The detective looked at her thoughtfully. "It's too early to say who intended what. It's true that you came up with an idea, the women each did their part, and your boyfriend happens to work with the scoreboard. That's a lot of coincidences, don't you think?"

Caitlin paused. "Yes. It is. But I never meant that we would do it. The only thing I told Aaron was how much fun we had plotting against the coach and how it united us. I never asked him to do anything. He laughed when I told him. For Pete's sake, he's a serious engineering student from a small town. Do you really think he'd knock off an obnoxious coach? He was an athlete in high school. He knows coaches are fickle. He just shrugs it off when I complain about the coach. He always says, 'You know, you can quit any time.'" She stopped, hands folded in her lap, and looked at Collins. "I should have listened to him."

"How was the coach with you? Did he pick on you?"

"He picked on everyone. Well, maybe not Annie. He had a favorite every year among the first-year students. Madison was it two years ago. See where that got her? He was the toughest on her lately. Last year it was Mary Johnson, who transferred out." Collins stirred in the chair. "Now it's Annie. It was never me, but I didn't mind. He was good enough my first two years. Not great, but not as bad as this year. He's been a total bully. He'd yell at me, sure, but not any more than anyone else. I didn't have a particular grudge against him, if that's what you're getting at."

"I'm not trying to 'get at' anything. Except the truth. And what went down with your team and your coach. Did you do your part of the plan?"

"Yes, but everyone did. I wasn't the only one."

"Can you think of anyone else who had a grudge against the coach? A boyfriend other than yours? A parent?"

"All of the parents have been pretty upset with the way he's been acting, but no one really stands out."

"What about the day of the coach's death? Did you see Aaron that afternoon?" Collins pressed.

Caitlin, looking startled, responded, "I told you, he was in the engineering lab all afternoon."

"Curious. I found him on a surveillance camera across campus from the lab, near the gym, during the time he said he was in the lab. He told me he had lunch with you. Did you lie about that?"

"I never lied. You didn't ask me about lunch. And lunch was much earlier in the afternoon than the coach's death. I wasn't trying to hide anything."

"Are you saying you did have lunch with Aaron?"

"Yes, I did. We met over at the student union."

"What time was that?"

"I'm not exactly sure."

"Give me your best guess," Collins pressed.

"I'd say about 1:00. The game was at 4:00. I can't eat too late or I get stomach cramps while we're playing. And I can't eat too early or I'm starving by the time the game is over."

"Where is the student union in relation to the gym?"

"It's a few buildings away. It's closer to the academic buildings."

Collins said, "Good to know. I might have more questions for you later."

Annie was next, and Collins was interested in meeting with her. "I understand you were the coach's pet."

Startled, she asked, "What do you mean?"

"I hear you were one of his favorites. Is that true? And why would that be?"

Annie blushed. "Well, the coach put me in for Madison pretty regularly. She's a junior and I'm a freshman. That's always hard. I guess some of the women felt he was playing favorites, but I thought I was at least as good as Madison. Sometimes better, sometimes not as good. He'd put her in, pull her, put me in. At the last game, he really reamed me out good. So, no, I don't—didn't—feel like I'm immune from his temper tantrums." Her hands moved nervously as she emphasized past tense.

"Did you participate in the pulling of the pins?"

"Not really. I was madder at myself than at him. He was right. I was playing awful. And he put me in for Madison whose folks and boyfriend were there from Mandan. She was pissed at all of us."

"Yeah," Collins said, "Mandan is a fair drive from here. I'm sure Madison and her family were disappointed. Do you think her father was mad enough to do something about it?"

"Oh no," Annie said, eyes widening in horror. "Her dad is a great guy. I can't believe he'd ever harm anyone."

"Who do you think killed the coach?"

"I don't know. I don't have any ideas."

"Was your father angry with him?"

"My dad? He wouldn't hurt a flea. Sure, the coach ticked him off sometimes, and he'd let him know he was upset. But kill him? No way." Annie looked at Lt. Collins with alarm.

"Okay, but if anything comes to you, please let me know, okay?"

An hour and a half later, he had finished his interviews. When he met with Carley, he said, "Well, their stories are pretty consistent. They hatched a plot to get even, mostly to make themselves feel better about what a jerk the coach had been to them. I'm hard pressed to think it was this group of women, but I'm not ruling it out yet. There aren't any other lead suspects, and it's a very eerie coincidence between what they dreamed up and what happened. Of the young women, Caitlin is of greatest interest. It was her idea, and her boyfriend works the scoreboard. I plan to talk with Annie's father, too. If you have any other ideas, please let me know."

Carley agreed. "I know. It's as if someone overheard them and saw an opportunity. But they were out of town. Some of the parents came, but not many. I can't believe anyone overheard the team talking and decided to implement such a hairbrained scheme."

"Well, *you* overheard the team in a hotel room. So we know it can happen. I need a list of the parents who were there. Can you get that for me?"

Carley choked, "I don't believe it was any of them or their families. Period."

"I know. You want to believe the best in all of them. Just get me the list. We'll know soon enough."

52

After practice the next day, Carley asked Hanna, "Do you have a few minutes to talk today?"

"Sure. What's the topic?" Hanna asked, as they walked into Carley's office.

"I understand you talked with Detective Collins about which players were the coach's favorites."

Hanna blanched. "I did. He asked me. Wasn't I supposed to?"

"Of course. You gave him good information. Would you mind telling me? Who were his favorites, and how did he act around them?"

"He always liked me, but he was a little distant. I know he liked Madison the first year she was on the team. He'd mess up her hair on the bus after a good game and harass her a little. But that wore off. He liked Annie and always held her up as the one to be like, even though she wasn't the strongest player. She certainly wasn't better than Madison, but she got more playing time. That's about it this year. Mary Johnson was his favorite last year. Usually, it was a freshman. He always gave his favorite more playing time."

"Did he do anything out of the ordinary with Mary Johnson or Annie? He messed up their hair? Is that one of the ways he singled out young women?"

"I hadn't thought about it like that, but yeah. It was like they were special to him. He wanted to make them laugh."

"Did he? I hate having my hair played with. I know that would bug me."

"Oh, he did it to tease them, which was part of his approach. It was weird, but none of us gave it much thought."

"And he never did that with you?"

"No, he wouldn't dare. My father and three brothers were always in the stands," Hanna said with a smile.

"Well, thanks. That's all I wanted to know."

After Hanna left, Carley called Madison on her cell phone. "Would you mind stopping by before practice tomorrow? I have a quick question for you." Madison indicated she would. Next, Carley called Annie and asked her to stop by her office after practice. Hesitantly agreeing, Annie asked what she wanted to discuss.

"I just want to make sure everything's going okay with you," Carley said.

The next afternoon Madison breezed in, "Hi, Coach. What's up today? Any more surprises for the team?"

"No," Carley said solemnly. "I know you've been upset with me about this whole business. I couldn't not say something. That would make me complicit. That's not in me. I do believe the team's story, and I understand why each girl did her part. The coach was a jerk. He was terrible to almost everyone. That's what I wanted to ask you. I know you were his favorite your freshman year. You got a lot of playing time, he teased you, he made you the center of attention. Is that fair to say?"

"Hmmm. I guess so. I didn't ask for any special attention. I just wanted to play."

"I understand he would tease you after a good game, ruffle your hair, sing a song to you. How did you feel about all that?"

"Oh," Madison said. "I *hated* it. It was embarrassing. I didn't want him to act like I was something special."

"Did you do anything about that? Did you say anything to him?"

"I did. One day I'd just had enough, and I kind of bit his head off in front of the other players to make him stop. He stopped, but it seemed like it pissed him off."

"How did he act toward you after that?"

"Well, Annie joined the team. Once she was here, I was toast. He put her in for me all the time."

"Did you feel like he was getting even because you rebuffed him?"

"It was only teasing, and I told him to stop. He did. End of story. He just thought Annie was a better player, and I couldn't convince him otherwise. I'm sure it didn't help that I yelled at him, but I don't think that's why he started putting Annie in. Why do you ask?"

"I think your coach really picked on some young women, and it seemed like you became one of them. Obviously, not right away. Did he ever try anything else with you?"

"No way. I wouldn't have let him. Even if he wanted to, I'm sure he knew that. I'm pretty tough."

"Well, thanks for chatting. I'm glad it was nothing. Let's go into practice," Carley said as she handed Madison a clipboard with stats.

When practice was over, Carley cornered Annie, "You're stopping by my office, right?"

Annie nodded, "But I don't have a lot of time."

"We'll make it work," Carley responded.

As they sat down, Carley asked Annie, "How do you think things are going with the team?"

"All right, I guess. We're playing better, finally. You're a good coach and so much easier on the team than Coach Pearson was. If we didn't have all this stuff hanging over our heads, we could enjoy it more."

"I understand. You're doing well."

"I got a lot more playing time with Coach Pearson. But I know it takes a while to sort out what the best combination of players is."

"Were you close to the coach?" Carley asked.

"I don't know. He seemed pretty happy with me until he wasn't. That was recent. He wasn't really happy with anyone."

"Did he ever embarrass you? Tease you in public? Sing to you on the bus?"

"Why do you ask," Annie asked, an uneasy tone in her voice.

"Well, I've been learning a few things about this coach that I've found pretty disconcerting."

"Like what?"

"It seems that every year he picked a new freshman to lavish attention on. That girl would get a lot of playing time. He had a pattern of embarrassing her on the bus in front of her teammates, but doing it in a way that made it uncomfortable for her to challenge him. In at least one case I know of, the coach pressed for more."

"What do you mean?"

"He wanted something in return, sexual favors, a pledge of love, intimacy. Something no coach has the right to want from a player. I've heard enough about how he treated you that I'm concerned he might have put you in a very difficult situation. And that worries me for you. It worries me that he's hurt you and that this may have affected you in ways that you don't even know yet. This is not your fault, Annie. He was a predator. If he did this to you, I want to support you, get you some help, make sure you're okay."

Annie didn't move. Her face paled, and her eyes seemed even grayer and more distant. Then she exploded into tears. "Why can't you just leave me alone?" she pleaded as she leapt to her feet, running out of Carley's office.

Carley jumped up to go after her, then knew she needed to let her go. She had the answer she was looking for, just not in the way she had hoped. What a terrible legacy this coach had left in his wake.

53

Mark gave Carley a quick call as she was driving back from Fargo that afternoon. "Hey, I'm going to Fargo for a high school volleyball tournament in a little while. Want to come along? Maybe you could do some recruiting."

"Actually, that's part of my job. I haven't had any time for that yet, so, sure. I'm on my way home. Are you at the lake, or should I turn around and meet you in town? I'd love to go with you. Is your stepdaughter playing?"

"Madelyn? Yes. She's a freshman and pretty good. Of course, I'm biased. Her father will be there, too, most likely. We all get along well. I'm at the lake. Want to ride in with me?"

"I have some interesting developments to tell you about," she said.

"I can only imagine. I'll look forward to hearing about them. See you in a few minutes," he responded.

As they headed back toward Fargo, Carley was relieved to have a chance for conversation with Mark. "Well, I got an answer today."

"What kind of an answer?" Mark asked as they sped down the two-lane road winding between small lakes and clumps of trees.

"I found out exactly how depraved the coach was."

"Oh, no. You've found another victim."

"Yes, one victim and one whom he wanted to have as a victim."

"Oh, geez. Have you told Pete yet?"

"I will. I'd like to get her to tell him first. Otherwise, I think she'll see it as a total betrayal."

He glanced over at her. "You can try to get her to speak up. My guess is she won't show up for practice any more. But if she won't tell the police, it's your responsibility, as a coach. You're considered a 'mandatory reporter' for sex abuse if the individual is underage or in a power relationship like coach/player."

Letting out a big sigh, Carley said, "You know, I didn't get much training for this coaching position. They just threw me into it, thinking my athletic background and play experience would be enough. I feel like I'm over my head, way beyond my pay grade here."

"For sure, murder is beyond your pay grade. Everything else pretty much comes with the territory. You'll learn," Mark consoled her. Carley rolled her eyes.

Carley continued, looking out the passenger window. "I think the school will be lucky not to get a lawsuit out of this. I'd sue if I were one of the parents. I talked with the athletic director who pooh-poohed the coach's behavior. I was shocked that, in this litigious world, the coach wasn't fired for sexual impropriety. The women were aware things weren't right. I don't know why the coach was so angry this year, but he had a pattern of finding a vulnerable freshman and preying on her. One of the women was just too strong and told him to stop it. But the others seemed glad for the attention, glad for the playing time, glad to be on his radar. Until it became too much."

"The athletic director should be fired."

"I'm betting he will be when the scope of what the coach did is really understood. I can't imagine the president standing for this. I think I'd better let him know the rest of what I've learned," Carley said.

"Pete will be concerned both for the girl and about anyone else she might have told who might have tried to get even—a boyfriend, a father, a brother. Do you think that might have happened here?"

"I don't know. She wouldn't talk with me about it. Would she tell a male in her life? My intuition says 'no.'"

"Well, I trust that intuition. It's generally pretty spot on."

"Except when I first met you. I thought you were a jerk," Carley reminded him.

"I had lied to you about who I was, after all. So you had reason to think that." They both chuckled, reminiscing about their early, off-putting encounters.

Carley became quiet for the rest of the drive. Knowing she was exhausted, Mark didn't press any further about what her next steps would be.

Luckily, the game was energetic. Madelyn's team won the first set by just three points and the second set by two. They lost the next two sets, but came back roaring in the fifth to win the match. Afterwards, Madelyn came running over to Mark and gave him a big hug. "Hi, Sweetie," he said, looking at her fondly. "You played awesome."

"Thanks, Mark. Is this Carley? I hear you're a volleyball coach at State."

"Yes, and in a few years, I'll be recruiting you," Carley said, smiling.

A tall, good-looking man came over and shook Mark's hand. "Good to see you, Mark. I'm glad you could come. It means a lot to Madelyn. You must be Carley. I've heard so much about you. I even read about you in the paper. I'm Charlie, Madelyn's dad."

Carley blushed, remembering the article in the paper about her abduction last summer. "Your daughter is really a good player. Sometime you should bring her over to State to watch the college women play. She's got the potential to play at that level."

Charlie nodded that he would. A mother of another player came jogging up the group. "Good game, Maddie," she said. Then, extending her hand to Mark said, "Hi, I'm Gloria. I don't think we've met. But I've heard all about you from my daughter. You're Maddie's 'other father,' right?"

Mark nodded, smiling.

"Sometime, when you come to a game, we should all go out for a bite to eat," she said, motioning in the general direction of Charlie and Mark. While she smiled at Carley, she made no attempt to include her in the invitation.

Carley felt a little pang of jealousy that surprised her. She had never felt jealous of anyone with Mark. But Gloria was darling, with dark, curly hair and deep-set eyes. What if someone swooped in and took Mark away? She swallowed hard.

The ride back to the lake was quiet and a little somber. Both Mark and Carley were tired after watching the exuberance in the gym. Plus, Carley was still reeling from her earlier conversation with Mark about what she was required to report to the police. She needed to get to Annie before she told Collins. She was quite sure Annie would never forgive her if she didn't.

54

Carley left her third message in two days. "Please, Annie, we need to talk further. This is not your fault. I am required legally to tell authorities what happened, or at least what I think happened to you and others on the team. I'd rather have you involved. Please, please talk to me."

She didn't know what else to do. Annie hadn't responded to her phone or text messages. Carley was afraid she might drop out of school and didn't want that to happen. Perhaps State's president could help her understand, though Carley was quite sure he would rather not be directly involved with this issue. Someone, however, had to be.

She sat at her desk, tapping her pencil, staring vacantly ahead. Suddenly, an idea came to her, and she jumped to her feet. Why hadn't this occurred to her earlier?

She jogged over to the Athletic Director's office, which was located in the administration building adjacent to the gym. When she walked into his office, she was greeted by Kristina, Brad's office manager. "Hey, Carley, how are things going in the world of volleyball?"

Carley smiled at Kristina warmly, "Oh, it hasn't been easy. But the women are great, and I trust things will settle down eventually. If they don't, well, that's another matter. I have a quick question for you. I haven't arranged transportation yet for away games. That was already done when I came into this role. How do I do that?

Whom do I go through and who usually drives the bus? Is there just one driver or are there several?"

Kristina had a narrow sheet of paper with phone numbers next to her phone. Quickly scanning she said, "Here's the number. It's under the department of transportation. Jed can help you. He has several regular drivers. Sometimes, when it's really a busy weekend, he'll hire a couple of extras."

"Do you know if he ever hires students or parents of team members to drive?"

"Oh, I doubt that. Liability, you know."

"Okay. Thanks, Kristina. I'll get in touch with Jed about the game coming up in Duluth."

Excusing herself, Carley pulled out her cell phone and called the number Kristina had given her. Jed answered. When she explained why she was calling, he said, "Let me look at the schedule. I think Coach Pearson had already given us that date."

A couple of minutes later he returned to the phone. "Yep, I've got you down. The bus will leave at noon on Friday, the 16th."

"Oh, you've already made the arrangements. Great! Who's the driver?" Carley asked.

"It's Bill Shepherd. He's a good one. Of course, we don't hire any bad ones," he chuckled.

"I've met Bill. He took us to the Brookings match a couple of weeks ago. Is he assigned to our team?"

"No, we don't do it that way. It depends where the team is going and how long they'll be gone. Some of the guys don't like to stay overnight. Others are more flexible."

"Do you know who drove the bus to our tournament in Illinois in early September? That was before I started."

"According to this list, that would have been Bill."

"Does he work on campus?"

"Sure. When he isn't driving the bus, he's a janitor for the administration building. He should be over there now. Is there something you want to talk with him about?"

"I wanted to ask him how the women were acting that weekend. If he talked to them at all. If he knows what parents were there. If he saw anyone unusual in the stands."

"Great. I'm sure he'd be happy to help you."

Immediately, Carley headed over to the administration building, but it wasn't easy to track Bill down. Finally, she found him on the third floor near a supply closet. Introducing herself, she explained she was looking for a little information about the trip to Illinois.

"I didn't drive the bus that weekend. Originally, I was scheduled to, but my mother got sick and needed some help. So I negotiated with Jed to find someone else. Let's see…I think it was Vic who drove for that trip."

Carley was pleasantly surprised by that. She didn't know Vic drove the team bus, but figured it could be helpful that he did. He would recognize most of the parents and could tell her if there were any new or unfamiliar faces in the crowd. She wondered if he knew Annie's dad and if he had noticed he was upset with the coach.

Finding Vic wasn't difficult. As usual, he was pushing the broom with cleaning compound across the gym floor.

"Hey, Vic," Carley called out.

"Hey, Coach," Vic smiled back at her. "How's life treating you? I'm glad you're back here at State. Those women are lucky. Are you having fun?"

"Well, fun isn't exactly the first word that comes to mind. Say, I wanted to ask you about the trip to Illinois—the one where you drove the bus because Bill Overland's mother was ill. Do you remember that trip?"

He stopped working, leaned over his broom and said, "Sure. I remember. I don't drive as much as I used to, and I really enjoy it when I do. Why? What do you need to know?"

"Did many parents show up for that game? I know we usually have a fairly good turnout, even for away games."

He nodded. "Oh, those parents are dedicated. They really have fun watching their daughters. I don't know if I can exactly remember, though. That was about a month and a half ago. And, you know, I'm getting old. My memory isn't as sharp as it used to be." He paused for a minute. "There were about eight parents as I recall."

She held up the photo of the mystery man. "What about this guy? Have you seen him around at any of the games? And did he come to Illinois?"

Vic's face flushed, and he stiffened. "Yeah, I've seen that guy around here. He wasn't at the Illinois game. I don't like him. I think he's up to no good. But I can't prove it. He was a pal of Coach Pearson."

"How about Annie's dad. Does he show up for games?"

"Yeah, he's a regular. Nice enough guy. A bit of a temper. Paces a lot lately."

"Like he's mad?"

"Maybe. I dunno." Vic paused. "You mean, was he mad at the coach? Oh, he'd yell at him all right. Sometimes he seemed pretty out of sorts, bluster with some of the other parents. He's a big guy, pretty intimidating. He's very protective of his daughter."

"What do you mean, protective?"

Vic thought for a moment. "He'd get in the coach's face if he didn't like the way he was coaching."

"Was he at the Illinois game?"

"Yeah, he was. He wasn't happy about how things were going."

"Did you see him talk with the coach?"

"I did. Don't know what he said, but he was upset. It was after the game."

Carley thanked Vic and headed out to her car. *If I were Annie's father and had any inkling what was up, I'd be angry, too,* she thought to herself.

55

It was the night of their big rival game, and the crowd was electric. The band was playing, something it rarely did for their sport, the cheerleaders were cheering, and the parents were hooting for their daughters. As Carley looked across the stands, she got a glimpse of Mark with his stepdaughter, Madelyn, and her father, Charlie. She waved big at the trio, marveling at how comfortable all three looked, and got a stand-up wave in return. Then she heard a group calling her name. Sitting near Mark was a group of outrageously dressed women, sporting the school colors and holding signs for "Carley for Coach of the Year," "This Team Rocks," "Go Team, Go." As she looked closer, she recognized nine women from her book club. Blushing, she waved vigorously at them as well. They shouted and cat-called back.

Annie was a no-show, as Carley expected. But the rest of the team appeared with their game faces on. Hanna and Brooke were pumped. Madison, assured of her spot with Annie gone, was completely reinvigorated. Juanita, the hot-shot libero, was hitting everything that came her way in warmups.

Once the ref blew her whistle, her team responded to the energy in the gym. Hanna was doing a great job calling plays, Brooke was slamming the ball into the court of their opponents, Madison was serving her all-time best. Carley couldn't have asked for more, especially in front of her audiences. Unfortunately, the other team was also motivated. In the end, her team fell three games to two, but the losses were narrow, and her team fought all the way. She had enjoyed all the cheering that came from her book club. What a great new group of friends they had already turned out to be.

When Mark came over to say goodbye to her, Carley gave Madelyn a hug. "I hope you enjoyed watching these young women play. You can be one of them some day."

Madelyn blushed, "Oh, I'd love that. I hope someday I'll be that good."

"Oh, you will be. Don't worry!" Carley nodded to Mark and Charlie.

Grabbing Mark by the sleeve, she asked, "Could I speak to you for just a minute?" Nodding, he walked her over to a corner of the court. "Did you learn anything about Derek Ericksen?" she asked.

"Yes, he finally showed up on one of our databases as a small-time drug dealer, not a big player, into a wide range of street drugs from steroids to meth to opioids. A couple of arrests, but no big possession charges. Most of his arrests were in Iowa, not Minnesota. I guess there's a big contingent of people from Iowa on Cormorant. If the coach were into drugs, I would bet he was the coach's supplier. I haven't heard back from Pete yet about whether or not they found any drugs in the coach's system. How about you? Anything new on your front?"

"I had an interesting conversation with the janitor today. Are you going straight home? Could I stop over for a minute after I get home?"

"Of course. I'll have something ready. Red wine or beer?"

"How about red wine tonight?" She said, smiling.

Mark nodded, grabbing her arm to give her a little tweak.

Before she left, she stopped by the locker room to congratulate the team on how well they played. "We didn't win," Brooke said, a pout on her lips.

"It's progress, all in the right direction. That's all we're looking for right now. Look at how well you fought!" She paused, then smiled at them. "Did you have fun?"

They all murmured, "Yes."

"Well, that's what matters the most."

On the dark drive back to her lake home, Carley reflected on the conversations she'd had that day, on the energy the young women put into the game, on the loss of Annie, on Annie's dad, and what Vic had said about him. Something was gnawing at her. She was glad she'd have a chance to talk with Mark. Then there was the way he had tweaked her arm. It was so genuinely affectionate. She smiled.

Mark met her at the door, poured wine glass in hand. "Madam Athlete," he said to her, as he waved his arm toward the small living room.

"Oh, that's a welcome sight," Carley said.

They sat down and discussed the game plays. In spite of having never played, Mark knew a fair amount about the game because of his stepdaughter, "I love that feisty libero. And Hanna and Brooke look like Mutt and Jeff, but they play together like a well-oiled machine. It won't be long before your team is winning again."

"Yes, but the season will be over by then," Carley commented dryly. It was frustrating how hard it had been to get them back on track.

"What did you want to discuss?"

"I found out an interesting thing today. The janitor, Vic, drove the team bus to Illinois, the place where the team hatched their scheme to get rid of the coach. I guess he's driven them before, but only once or twice. I asked him if he could recall any parents or boyfriends, and he said Annie's dad was there and that he's been doing a lot of pacing lately. Said he would get in the coach's face and was protective of his daughter. I've heard he has a short fuse. Vic also said he didn't notice the mystery man at that game, but he knew who I meant. Said he didn't trust him, though he couldn't elaborate why."

Mark said, "I can understand that. He looks shifty." He added, "I sent Pete the information about Derek Ericksen. I know he plans to talk with him as soon as possible. If he has an alibi that holds up, then it's more likely it's someone who really cares about a player.

Carley nodded in agreement. "By the way, thanks for bringing Madelyn to my game."

"It was fun. Charlie enjoyed it, too. I told him he should be thinking about how to encourage Madelyn's volleyball career. It might be a ticket to a big scholarship for her."

"Absolutely. I'm glad you enjoyed it. Really, this is a wonderful team," Carley said. "Say, whatever happened with Gloria? Have you three gotten together for a celebration?"

Mark looked puzzled. "Gloria? Oh—you mean that pushy mom who wanted to organize a dinner and wasn't about to include you?" he said with a smirk.

"Yeah. That one." She was impressed that Gloria's snub hadn't gone unnoticed.

"I'm too busy to make time for her. After all, we have a case to solve," he said, looking squarely into her eyes.

Somehow, Carley felt relieved. She knew she didn't have a right to feel badly. They were just friends, after all. But it made her feel better just the same. Finishing the glass of wine, Carley turned to Mark. "Thank you for all you're doing for my team. I know you're doing it for me."

"Well, I'm glad that hasn't escaped you," he laughed, with a nod.

Meanwhile, the man three cottages down watched her through his binoculars as she returned to her cottage. He didn't like how much time she was spending down the beach. Was she involved with this man? Didn't she know he wasn't right for her? She should be saving herself for him, after all. Just like he was saving himself for her.

56

The next night was the last meeting of the book club before some of them departed for the winter. The women moved so easily among themselves, Carley marveled. They had been friends a long time, and she the very grateful newcomer. One of the women approached her, "How are you doing with the scandal that's broken out at State? Your team is the epicenter of what's going on. That must be pretty hard on you."

Carley thought for a minute. *"Hard on you" is a relative concept,* she thought to herself. "The women have definitely taken it hard. It's affected their play all year. There are a lot of moving parts. In the end, the truth will win out, and we will all survive. In the meantime, THANK YOU for not deserting me! I loved having you come to the game. I will never forget your kindness," she said, tears welling up in her eyes.

"Are you kidding? We had a ball! Eileen here was an ace volleyball player during college, so she translated everything that was going on. You were pretty impressed with the caliber of players, weren't you, Eileen?"

"Absolutely! And it was fun watching you coach. You've got a strong connection with the women, even though you've only been coaching a few weeks. I'd come anytime. Let us know your game schedule."

Everyone nodded in agreement.

"I'd love to have you see a game we *win*," Carley said with a smile. "We haven't done much of that yet, but the women have a lot of talent."

"And we saw Mark Dolan at the game with his stepdaughter. Are you two an item?" one of the women asked.

"No. We're just friends. He saved my life this summer when I was kidnapped. I owe him a lot. But no, we're like brother and sister. I suggested he bring his stepdaughter because she's interested in volleyball." Carley could feel her face getting warm.

"I don't know—he's pretty cute," one of them smirked.

"Oh, leave the poor woman alone. She's had enough of men for a while," Eileen spouted.

Carley looked at her gratefully. Yes, she'd had enough of men to last a long time. But she was glad they noticed him. It meant so much to her that he'd brought Madelyn to the game.

From there, the discussion turned to the newest mansion going up on Pelican Lake, what was in the delicious casserole one of the women brought, and how to take on a school superintendent. Eventually, they even discussed the book briefly. Carley loved this group and looked forward to getting to be closer friends with several of them. And, despite the age difference, Betty Sue was the one with whom she felt the greatest kinship. She missed having a mother-like person in her life. It was also fun to hear them talk about Mark, who had caught their attention.

Were she and Mark really "just friends?" That seemed like such an inadequate way to describe him. He had become such an important part of her life. After Gordon, she wanted to swear off men for a long time. But she understood more now about why she fell for him. And why she fell for Mac. She had moved in with Mac shortly after her father's death. She could remember how adrift she felt at the time, and Mac seemed to be a safe harbor. *Obviously, I'm a poor judge of safe harbors,* she thought to herself. Gordon was tied to her father, too. He talked about what a mentor her father had been to him, when, in reality, her father had fired him. Had she known anything about his past, had her father ever mentioned him, her antennae would have been up from the start. However, she naively felt her deceased father had sent him her way. Both men had betrayed her trust.

Mark wasn't like either of them. She trusted him deeply and it was important to him that she knew she could. They had such an intimate relationship, without being physically intimate. Was it better not to have sex get in the way?

57

The next day, Pete, Mark, and Carley met for a cup of coffee and a quick update.

"I've found a few helpful things," Collins said. "The drug testing came back positive. There were strong traces of opioid use, but everything else—meth, heroin, performance enhancing drugs—all came back negative. According to his medical records, the coach had some sports-related injuries about three years ago that resulted in back trauma. He had been treated with opioids for a while, but the physician switched him to non-opioid drugs for pain control. They're never as effective, and I'm sure he was addicted. Oxy is a powerful drug. He had to have a supplier."

"Likely it was Derek Ericksen. Have you talked to him?" Mark asked.

"Already did. I went over to his place yesterday. He seemed very uneasy and said they were fishing buddies. Said he was at the casino in Mahnomen the afternoon the coach died. I've checked, and his player's card was used then. That doesn't mean he was there; he could have given it to someone else to use. But it's not likely. I'm getting video from the casino to see if I can verify what he said. It'll take a few days," Collins said. "I'm not feeling it with him. A creep, yes. Probably a minor drug supplier, yes. A murderer, I don't know. I just don't see the motive. I've gotten ahold of the coach's financials, and they're not bad. He had money to pay off a drug debt, so I'm thinking that's not what this was about."

"Are you thinking it comes back to the young women or someone close to them?" Carley asked.

"Yes, we still haven't ruled out the boyfriend—Aaron. He's still our top candidate right now. We don't know if there was an angry parent or brother or boyfriend who discovered what was happening, besides Mary Johnson's and Annie's dads. There could be someone else there. But the coincidence with the women's plot is just too close for comfort for me."

"Should we notify parents about what's going on? Let them know their daughters are in jeopardy unless someone steps forward?" Carley asked.

"We're not required to because these young women are all eighteen or older. But I'm sure they would appreciate a heads up. I could send an email letting them know what's going on," Collins said. "Do you think any of the parents know about their daughters' scheme?"

"It's possible, but no one has come to talk with me about it," Carley said.

"Maybe we need to turn up the heat," Collins suggested.

"Worth a try," Mark echoed.

"I can help here, too," Carley added. "Just tell me what to do."

"First, do you have any parent photos? And do you have email addresses for the parents?"

"Yes to both," Carley replied.

"I'll work on that email," Collins said. "I'll be back in touch."

58

Pete Collins sat down with Vic near the Facilities office on campus. Looking over pictures of the players and their families, Vic pointed to four sets of parents, "I'm pretty sure these eight were at the Illinois tournament. These four haven't missed a game yet. And their daughters are seniors now," he said, pointing to Hanna's and Brooke's parents.

"How about these four? Whose parents are they? I don't know the names of all the players," he said.

"These two are Madison's parents. She's a hotheaded little thing. Comes with the red hair. The other two are Annie's parents. She's a freshman so I don't know her parents as well. They make it to most of the games. Her dad can be pretty intense."

"Can you think of any others?" Collins asked gently.

"I've been wracking my brain. These are the only ones I can think of. All the parents come if the game is in Fargo. We have such great support from parents. But not as many come to a tournament that's out-of-state like this one was."

"You mentioned that one of the players is short-tempered. Are any of the parents?"

"There are always one or two who get pretty nasty toward the coach or the ref. These four are pretty laid back," Vic said, pointing to the parents of Hanna and Brooke. "Madison's parents don't get to many games, and they usually mind their p's and q's. But I've seen them get upset at how Madison's treated. Like I said, Annie's parents I don't know as well. As I recall, the father does a lot of yelling, but that doesn't mean anything."

"Did he get ever in the coach's face?"

"Yes, though I couldn't overhear what he was saying. He wasn't happy about something."

"Was he mad at the coach in Illinois?"

"Yeah. He looked pretty fed up. Went and talked with the coach face-to-face. I thought it was a risky move because the coach could take it out on his daughter. But he didn't seem to care. He blustered at him a bit. Looked like he'd like to punch him, but he didn't."

"Did any boyfriends come to this tournament?"

"I don't really know their boyfriends. They might have been there, and I wouldn't have known. Oh, except for Aaron. He works on the scoreboard so I know him. He's Caitlin's boyfriend. He was there."

"Did you talk to any of the young women after the tournament?" Collins asked.

"Nah, they were pretty upset. Just got on the bus and put their headphones on. It's a lot more fun when things go well," Vic acknowledged.

"Thanks, Vic. If you think of anyone else, would you please give me a call? I'd be grateful," Collins said.

"Sure 'nuf."

Pete sent a text to Carley and Mark a few moments later. *Four sets of parents were at the Illinois tournament. Vic identified one as having a short fuse: Annie's father. Wasn't she the other girl you were concerned about?*

Carley shook her head as she read his text. Annie. There she was again. The only other one she could identify that the coach came on to, besides Mary. Did Annie's father know something wasn't right? Did she believe he would take any action, especially such dramatic action, against a coach? Nothing stood out in her previous interactions with Annie's family. Might Hanna know if something had gone down that weekend?

She texted Hanna, asking her to meet in her office for a few minutes when she could. Before she knew it, Hanna was in her doorway, "I got your text as I was coming into the building, so I thought I'd just keep coming," Hanna said with a smile. "What do you need?"

"I have a question I'd like to ask you, and I'd like you to keep it just between us. Do you mind?"

Hanna nodded she would.

"What do you know about Annie's family? Does her father fly off the handle easily?"

"Sometimes. I don't think he cared much for the coach," Hanna said, her brow furrowed.

"Were parents upset at the Illinois tournament?"

"No more than usual. My parents thought the coach was rude. But they also didn't want to make waves that could hurt me. I didn't see anybody out of control, if that's what you're wondering."

"Yeah, that's exactly what I was wondering. Vic said there were four sets of parents who were there."

"That sounds about right. It was out-of-state, so it was harder for families to attend. Most of us were glad we didn't have a bigger audience. We played like shit."

"Where did they stay?"

"In the same hotel we were at. Usually, the hotels give a discount for teams and their families."

"Do they stay on the same floor as the team?"

"No, they try to keep us separate. Plus, the parents are usually drinking, and they don't want that to rub off on us," Hanna said, chuckling.

"Thanks. That's all I needed to know. I appreciate you stopping by."

"Any time, Coach," Hanna said, picking up the heavy load of books she'd set down. "Ugh. Chemistry. My load will be a lot lighter after that class is done. I almost lost this book in Illinois," she said, pointing to the largest of the bunch. "I left it on the bus. Fortunately, or maybe unfortunately, Vic rescued it for me," she said, bouncing out of the office.

Carley thought to herself, *I'd like Vic to drive to all of our out-of-town games.* She decided she'd try to make that happen.

59

Lt. Collins walked into the front office of the large construction company owned by Jim Benson. A receptionist looked up, smiled, and asked whom he was there to see. A few minutes later, a tall, bulky, middle-aged man, shirt sleeves rolled up, emerged from one of the back offices. "Lt. Collins, I'm Jim Benson. Please, come back into my office."

The building smelled of concrete, cigarettes, and coffee. Jim motioned to Lt. Collins to sit down across from his desk, which was covered with blueprints, file folders, two empty cans of diet coke, and a full ashtray. "How can I help you?"

"As I told you when I phoned, I'm investigating the death of the volleyball coach, Pearson, at State. Your daughter, Annie, is on his team. I wanted to learn more about your connection to him."

"He was my daughter's coach. That's my only connection to him," Benson said, staring Lt. Collins in the eye.

"I've been told you didn't care much for him. Is that true?"

"Who told you that?"

Lt. Collins shrugged. "You know I can't reveal my sources. I hear you were pacing at the games. Yelling at the coach. Tell me how you felt about the man."

"I didn't care for him. I didn't like the way he treated the girls. I didn't like the way he treated Annie. I don't know. There was something too intense about him. I thought he crossed the line."

"And what line would that be?"

"Good coaching behavior. He was too hard on everyone. Yelled at them. Kept them off balance. It was like he was into mind control."

"Did you have any reason to believe he was coming on to any of the players? Coming on to your daughter?"

"Whaaat? No. Oh God, no, he wasn't doing that, was he? Did he come on to Annie? She never said anything like that."

"Did you ever ask her?"

"Why would I? It didn't really cross my mind. My daughter is beautiful. I give you that. I've always worried about guys coming on to her. But the coach? I would have busted his balls."

"Didn't you wonder why she got so much playing time as a freshman? Was she really better than the other players? Even as good as the other players? Didn't you ever notice him put his arm around her shoulder?"

Benson became very quiet. *Of course you did,* Collins thought to himself.

"Where were you the afternoon the coach was killed?"

"I don't know. I'll have to do some checking. Most likely I was right here, where I usually am. And driving to the game. The stadium is a good hour away from Detroit Lakes."

"Can anyone verify you were here?"

"I'll have to check. I'm usually here alone on Saturdays. I think it's time you left now. Next time, I want my attorney to be present."

Collins got up to leave. "You have a very interesting business here. You have access to a lot of equipment that could have been used to bring the scoreboard down. The coach may have been coming on to your daughter. We've been trying to get that question answered. Your alibi will be pretty important. And you'll have to be able to prove it."

Benson jumped to his feet, motioning toward the door. "I'm sure you can find your way out.

60

The next morning in her office, Carley opened an email from Collins addressed to her and Mark. Derek Ericksen's alibi held up. Footage from the casino cameras showed he'd been there when he said he was. And Mahnomen was far enough way to make it impossible for him to have slipped out and back. One of the blackjack dealers recognized him as a regular and said he was a jerk, always using foul language, bragging, harassing other players. He couldn't remember much about that night.

Carley closed her laptop. It was likely whoever murdered the coach not only knew him, but also knew what was going on and wanted revenge. How glad she would be when this was over. Collins was talking with Annie's father that day. Father, brother, boyfriend—did any of them know what was happening between Annie and the coach?

Wishing she could connect with Annie, Carley called the registrar's office and got Annie's class schedule. She'd wait for her outside of her next class, which ended in about half an hour. She was out of options.

She stood outside the classroom door, waiting for Annie to emerge. Students poured out—about thirty of them. Disappointed none of them were Annie, Carley poked her nose into the classroom to see if anyone was left. There stood Annie, looking at a paper with the instructor, oblivious to anyone around her. Carley quickly stepped back out to wait for her when she emerged.

Ten minutes later, Annie came, folding her paper and cramming it into her backpack, which she hoisted over her shoulder. Startled to see Carley, she put her head down and kept on going. Carley quickly caught up with her. "Annie, please, stop. Talk with me. I don't want to do anything that would hurt you. I don't want to know any details of what happened with you unless you want to share them. I just want to make sure you're okay."

"I'm okay, all right? Now, please, won't you leave me alone?" Annie said with irritation in her voice. "I have to get to my next class."

Carley kept up, talking quietly. "What the coach did was wrong, and I'm very worried that you blame yourself. He was a manipulator—and that's exactly how he wanted you to feel. It's not your fault. I don't care what you think. When a coach has so much power over a player, boundaries are critical. He didn't have any with you. Please, please, please just know I want to make this right for you."

Annie stopped in her tracks. "There is no way to make things right for me. My teammates will know that the only reason I got so much playing time was because I caved with the coach. They won't respect me. My parents would be furious if they knew."

"We can keep this confidential. I can see to that. I have someone I'd like you to talk with. She's an expert in things like this. The team doesn't know about this, and I know you're a good player. We can keep it hush hush."

"I don't believe you. I know the police are involved. If this gets out…," her voice trailed off and she looked off into the distance, her eyes narrowing.

"I've already told the police what I think happened to you. Of course, it would be much better if they heard it from you."

"Better for whom? I don't want to talk about this anymore." She was radiating anger. Turning on her heel, she sprinted away from the direction they had been walking.

She doesn't seem to think her parents knew about the coach. This is clearly troubling her so deeply, how will she get over it without professional help? Carley thought to herself. She wished she could help Annie see that getting counseling would be the best thing she could do right now.

61

It was the middle of practice, and nothing was going well. Carley decided the team needed a little pep talk. Calling the young women to center court, she drew a deep breath. Then she spotted two people entering the gym. It was Lt. Collins and a female police officer she didn't recognize. She left the group to walk toward them. "Hello, officers. What can I do to help?"

Lt. Collins spoke first. "We're here on official police business, and I'd like you to not get in the way." They kept walking to where the team was standing, gawking. "Caitlin, we need you now."

Caitlin stepped tentatively toward the duo.

Lt. Collins said, "Caitlin, we are arresting you for the death of Coach Pearson. You have the right to remain silent. Anything you say can and will be used against you in a court of law. You have the right to an attorney. If you cannot afford an attorney, one will be provided for you. Do you understand the rights I have just read to you?"

Caitlin, a look of terror in her eyes, didn't speak.

Lt. Collins repeated, "Do you understand what I've just said?"

Caitlin nodded. "Can I please call my parents?"

"You can call them from the station."

"Why are you arresting only me?" Caitlin asked.

"We're not arresting only you. We've also arrested your friend, Aaron, and are charging you both with conspiracy to commit murder."

"Aaron didn't have anything to do with it. And why aren't you charging the entire team then? Everyone was in on it."

"Because we think you two were the main ones responsible."

The female officer approached Caitlin, asked her to turn around, and placed handcuffs around her wrists.

"Is this really necessary? Can't she just walk out of here?" Carley asked.

"We know what we're doing. Let us do our jobs," Collins responded. The officers led Caitlin to the waiting squad car.

The event sucked the air out of the gym. Carley was dumbfounded and angry that Lt. Collins hadn't given her a heads up. *He is such a cold fish,* Carley thought to herself. Was he worried she would tell Caitlin? And what should she do now?

"That was quite a shock." Carley surveyed the stunned faces surrounding her. Some of the girls had begun to cry. "I didn't know anything about this. I'll try to find out more. I think we're done for today," she said.

"Are all of us in jeopardy?" Hanna asked.

"I don't know any more than you do. You might want to let your parents know what just happened. I'll try to learn what went down, what evidence they have. This is pretty tough. Go back to your dorms and apartments. I'll let you know tonight what I find out."

The girls began to disperse, whispering anxiously to each other. Carley pulled out her cell phone to call Mark.

62

An hour later, back in her office, Carley slumped into her chair, her elbows on the desk, her head in her hands, her eyes closed. *How can this be happening?* Carley thought to herself. *Can Aaron and Caitlin really have pulled this off? Why? And what about Annie? How can I help her? This team is unraveling.* She had done everything she knew to do. Everything the expert in similar cases had advised her to do. What she really wanted was justice for Annie.

Absentmindedly, she picked up an envelope addressed to her on her desk, turning it over and over. Finally, realizing it hadn't been opened, she took Coach Pearson's letter opener, slit it open, and started reading, with dismay, what was inside.

It was a letter from Vic, in his handwriting, wobbly and hard to read. She leaned forward, frozen, gasping as she read:

Dear Missy,

I was sick watching the police take your player away. I couldn't let her take the fall for something she didn't do. The team is a special bunch, and they didn't deserve what the coach gave them. I've watched him all these years, watched him seduce the freshmen with playing time, watched him yell and scream when players didn't play well enough, watched him embarrass the girls in front of their families. It's a wonder any of them would play for him. I saw what he did to that Mary girl. He should have been arrested. I reported it to the athletic director, Brad, but he just told me to mind my own business. No one would stop him. I finally decided I needed to.

I overheard what the girls were plotting. I brought Hanna's chemistry book back to her room, and they were having a great time coming up with how they would bump off the coach. I didn't think anyone would believe they could do it or that it would work. I guess I wasn't thinking clearly. So I decided to make sure he got taken out of the way. I was the one who jimmied the score board. I was the one who rigged it so I could let it go when the coach was on the ref stand. I was the one who stopped him from hurting any more girls. The girls didn't have anything to do with it.

I know I shouldn't have done it. But I'm getting old, and I'm sick, and I just didn't want to leave, knowing this creep could keep on doing what he's done all these years. It isn't right. I don't mind dying. I haven't been well and don't have much time left, anyway. Don't feel badly for me, Missy. You're a great coach and someone the girls can look up to. I'm so proud of you—always have been. You know I watched you play since you were a freshman, and you were always one of the kindest, smartest people I knew. These girls need you. Give them everything you've got.

Sincerely,
Vic

Carley leapt to her feet, punching her speed dial for Mark as she ran out the door of her office. He didn't answer. Frantically, she called Collins, who said he would be right there. "Hurry," Carley said. "I think he's going to try to kill himself, if he hasn't already."

Jamming her phone into her pocket, Carley sprinted out of her office toward Vic's. It was locked and dark. Through the wavy glass she could see it was empty. She called campus security to enlist their help. And she called Brad, the athletic director, to tell him what was going on. Where could Vic be, and what danger was he in?

Security was there in minutes—three officers and the vice president to whom they reported. Everyone spread out, searching the bleachers, empty classrooms, and storage closets for any sign of Vic. In the distance, Carley could hear sirens. She was sure Collins was on his way. *What if they don't find Vic in time?*

Carley talked with the head of security, telling him about the contents of the letter and relaying her conversation with Vic from the previous day. "We need to find him. I'm afraid he's going to hurt himself," she said.

Collins showed up minutes later. "What do you know?" he asked as he came jogging over to Carley.

"Not much. We've searched the gym. He's not here."

"What about the steps up to the rafters? Where Vic took me to see the scoreboard anchors. Did anyone check that?"

Calling the head of security to go with them, they raced out of the gym, toward the door that led into the gym attic. The door was closed and locked. Security's master key worked, and the detective pulled down the ladder and moved quickly, almost recklessly, to the next landing. Carley followed. He pulled down the second set of stairs and scaled those, with Carley close behind. At the top, he took out his flashlight and scanned the expanse. No one was up there.

Back in the gym, Collins pulled the crew together, told them he had had a patrol car go to Vic's home to see if he was there, and asked if anyone knew any place he might have gone. His phone rang with the news that Vic wasn't in his apartment, and neighbors hadn't seen him all day. Collins asked, "We have to make sure we keep students safe. Do you have any ideas of other places he may have gone? Anywhere on campus?"

Everyone shook their heads. All of a sudden, Carley stopped, her face pale. "I have an idea." Running back to her office, she grabbed the photograph Vic had given her when she started coaching. "He said this was his favorite place to go with his wife when she was living. He took the photograph. It's on the Red River, and it's downstream from Dike West Park. Because the river flows north, it's north of the dike. I used to go there when I was a student."

"Come on, let's go. You can show me where it is," Collins said to Carley.

Jumping into his squad car, Carley texted a message to Mark. *Vic left me a note confessing to the murder. We're trying to find him, headed to the Red River in Fargo, probably on the bridge near the edge of downtown. If you can meet us there, would you?*

Collins called for back-up support and gave them approximate coordinates of where they would be. Flipping on his flashing lights and siren, he pulled out of the parking lot. Carley grabbed his arm and said, "I don't think we should go in like this. If he's there and alive, we'll want to try to talk him down." Collins looked at her for a second and flipped the lights and siren off.

It was a good call. As the squad car raced toward the river, Carley sat, shaking, afraid of what they might find when they arrived. She directed Collins to the overlook near the bridge and a boat landing where they could park. As Collins pulled to a stop, Carley jumped out of the squad car. Running to where the bridge met the river, Carley came to an abrupt halt. It was a chilly evening, and leaves were quickly falling off the trees and into the cold Red River below. The overlook rose above the river and there, at the point, stood Vic, staring at the depth below, clutching something firmly in his arms.

Carley motioned to the detective to follow her slowly. "I know him. He's a good man. Please, let me talk with him, will you?"

Collins paused, then nodded yes.

"And stay back here," Carley said, motioning him back with her hand. Collins looked less convinced about that, but stayed.

After getting within shouting range, Carley called out to Vic, "Vic, it's me. Missy. I got your letter, but please, please, please don't do anything foolish. You are such a good man. I know that about you. You did what you thought was right. Please, won't you come down so we can talk about this?"

Vic looked up, spotting Carley and Collins in the background. "Oh Missy, how did you know I'd be here? I'm sorry you found me. I didn't want you to find me."

"Oh, Vic," Carley pleaded, slowly taking small steps to get closer to him. "Please don't do this."

"I'm ready to die," Vic said. "My wife is gone, I have cancer, and I did a terrible thing. Why should I go on?"

"That's not true," Carley, now within ten feet of him, said more quietly. "You need to tell people what you know."

"I did what I needed to do. I wanted to save those girls from that predator. From that jerk. He was terrible, and they didn't deserve him. They deserve you, and I'm glad it's all come together the way it has."

"Vic," Carley implored him. "You and I have always been buddies. Be that buddy still. I don't want to lose you. You did a very risky thing to protect the girls. I'm so, so sorry that no one listened to you. I know what the coach did. I know about Mary and Annie, and I'm sure there were others."

Vic nodded, frowning.

"Just come down now, so we can talk. So you can tell us what you know about the coach. So we can help people understand why you did what you did."

"It doesn't matter, Missy. I don't want to do this to you, but I don't have much choice as I see it. Life just isn't worth living any more. I feel good about my work at the school. I loved my wife, and I got rid of someone who should have been gotten rid of years ago. I feel content. I don't want to go on any further. And I want you to stay back now."

Detective Collins stepped out of the shadow. "Please, Vic. I know you don't know me. But I heard what you did. It took a lot of guts. You really cared about those students. If you did, care about them now. Care about Carley. Please don't do this."

Vic just shook his head. "Just tell people I wasn't trying to be bad. I just had to stop him. He was an evil man. I couldn't stand it anymore. You be good, Missy, you hear?"

In one effortless move, he bent his head, kissed the picture clutched in his hand, and did a sailor dive—headfirst, body straight, arms tightly holding a Bible against his chest—off the bridge into the cold, muddy water of the Red River below. He fell silently and disappeared almost without a splash.

Carley and Collins raced to the edge of the embankment. Collins radioed for officers to see if they could find him. There was no sign of him. It was a long fall into cold water. Carley turned to step onto the path down to the water, but Collins pulled her back. "It's no use. You'll never get down there in time. He's gone."

Carley looked up and saw Mark sprinting toward them. She fell into his arms, sobbing.

63

Carley was somber as she started practice the next day. Her eyes swollen, her head throbbing, her mind numb, Carley stood in front of the team, tears on her cheeks. "He was a good man who saw evil in this gym. He tried to tell the authorities, but no one listened. He couldn't stand all of you being at risk, so he took justice into his own hands. He was a kind, gentle man who couldn't put up with what he saw happening. What he did was clearly wrong. And he's paid dearly for that. He loved all of us, and I hope that will be his legacy." Looking up, Carley was surprised to see Annie joining the circle the team was sitting in.

Annie looked around at the team. "I decided if he could risk everything for us, for me, I needed to show up and tell my story. Vic is my hero. I know he did something very wrong, but he did it to protect us. The same way I did something wrong, and I hope you will forgive me." As she started to sob, the team flocked around her, giving her a team hug as only a team can do.

Carley spoke again. "The good news is that it's over. You've all been cleared. I talked with Detective Collins this morning. While he will ask everyone to give a statement, he has dismissed you from any culpability," she finished. She gave a special nod to Caitlin, who fist-bumped Madison.

There was a collective sigh of relief in the room. Several of the young women began to cry quietly. "It's been a long fall," Hanna said. "Can we finally go back to having fun?"

Carley looked at each girl, "You've carried a big burden these past couple of months. I'm sure you've learned a lot from this experience. But I'm with you. It's been a hard time. Let's go have some fun. And let's always keep Vic in our hearts."

At the game that night, crowds poured into the gym. Some were thrill seekers, wanting to learn more about what happened. Many were parents and families who came to support their daughters and sisters. Many were students who came to support their friends. Some were faculty. And in the middle of all the commotion were twelve women, decked out in the school's colors, waving pompoms, and holding signs that read, "Go Team" and "We love you, Carley!" Her book club was there in full force, bringing tears to Carley's eyes. Nearby sat Mark.

The game was electric. Carley marveled to herself that she hadn't seen the women perform this well, even in past game videos. Brooke was hurling the ball into the other court. Hanna's sets were flawless. Madison's energy was unstoppable.

In the end, the women handily won all three sets. As they crowded around Carley after the game, sweat dripping, hearts pumping fast, Carley said to them, "Let's remember two men today. The coach who brought you here and the janitor who wanted to keep you safe."

Hanna joined in, "And the coach who kept us here. You." Together, they yelled, "Team," followed by hugs and more tears. They were back.

As the gym cleared, Carley greeted the crowd around her—the president, faculty and staff, parents, her book club—thanking them for their show of support and for not losing faith in the team or in her. Noticeably absent was the athletic director, fired that afternoon for gross negligence. As her friends and the fans flowed around her, one lone figure caught her eye.

Mark stood off on the sidelines, waiting for her, his hands in his pockets, smiling, enjoying the swell of people around her. Spotting him, Carley broke loose. Shaking her head lightly, she took a deep breath, then sprinted toward him. His smile widened. When she reached him, she threw her arms around him, hugging him hard, almost sending him reeling. Recovering quickly, he wrapped his arms tightly around her, holding her upright, laughing.

Pulling back so she could see his face, she met his eyes. "Once again, you showed up," Carley said. She paused, then said gently, "Thank you."

Mark pulled her toward him again and kissed her with a surprising, sensual, deep, lingering kiss. For a moment, they were alone in the emptying gym. Holding her gaze, he whispered, "Always." And they kissed again, months of confusion and restraint melting away.

Meanwhile, the man with the binoculars three doors down paced in his cabin. He'd been watching her for so long. He was certain she had no idea. He was in love with her. It was time for him to make his move. And he knew exactly how he wanted to make it. The question was, when? And what to do about this interloper who was taking all her time?

ACKNOWLEDGMENTS

Thank you to the many people who helped me develop this story:

- Those who generously read drafts and provided feedback, including Carl Brookins, Gail Wieberdink, Sandra Anderson, Cindy Burns, Shelly Franz, Marcia Leatham, and Peggy Malikowski.

- My niece, Tracey Trudeau, for your encouragement and expert editing skills.

- Betty Lou Scott, Roberta Lovell, Mary Kloster, and my sister, Marcia Rogers, for your unwavering support and cheerleading.

- Officer Anne Marie Buck, Hopkins Police Department, for input into police procedures.

- Evonne and George Lund for your expert advice on Big Cormorant Lake.

- My daughters, Jill and Laura, through whom I developed a love of volleyball.

- My partner, Rich Sherry, for your unwavering support, spectacular editing skills, word suggestions, and countless hours reviewing drafts. I could not have done this without your love and dedication.

- All who have given me encouragement along the way.

mystery
MANCE
2021

1705193 $15.95

Made in the USA
Columbia, SC
28 July 2021